The Moon Opera

Bi Feiyu

Translated from the Chinese by
Howard Goldblatt and Sylvia Li-chun Lin

Houghton Mifflin Harcourt

Boston · New York 2009

Bi

First published in English in 2007
by Telegram Books

For information about permission to
reproduce selections from this book, write to
Permissions, Houghton Mifflin Harcourt
Publishing Company, 6277 Sea Harbor Drive,
Orlando, Florida 32887-6777.

www.hmhbooks.com

Library of Congress Cataloging-in-Publication Data
Bi, Feiyu.
The moon opera / Bi Feiyu translated from the Chinese
by Howard Goldblatt and Sylvia Li-chun Lin.
p. cm.
Originally published: London : Telegram, 2007.
ISBN 978-0-15-101294-7
1. Women singers — China — Beijing — Fiction. 2. Opera
companies — China — Beijing — Fiction. I. Goldblatt,
Howard, date. II. Lin, Sylvia Li-chun. III. Title.
PL2931.5.I18M66 2009
895.1'352 — dc22   2008029358

Printed in the United States of America

Book design by Robert Overholtzer

1 2 3 4 5 6 7 8 9 10 DOC

The Moon Opera

ONE

FOR QIAO BINGZHANG the dinner party was like a blind date, and it was half over before he learned that the man sitting across from him ran a cigarette factory. Qiao was an arrogant man and the factory boss was even more so, which is why their eyes hadn't really met. One of the guests asked "Troupe Leader Qiao" if he'd been on the stage in recent years. Qiao shook his head; now the other guests realized that he was none other than Qiao Bingzhang, the celebrated *Laosheng* of the Peking Opera, who had been wildly popular in the early eighties, his voice heard on transistor radios day and night.

They raised their glasses in a toast.

"Actors these days," a guest quipped, "find their looks are a faster road to fame than their names, and their names will get them there quicker than their voices. Apparently, Troupe Leader Qiao was born at the wrong time!"

Bingzhang laughed agreeably.

"Isn't there someone called Xiao Yanqiu in your troupe?" the large, heavyset man across from him asked. Then, on the off chance that Qiao Bingzhang didn't know who this was, he added, "The one who played the lead role in the 1979 performance of *Chang'e Flies to the Moon — The Moon Opera.*"

Qiao Bingzhang set down his glass, shut his eyes, and then opened them slowly. "Yes, there is," he said.

Putting aside his arrogance, the factory boss talked the guest next to Bingzhang into switching seats with him, then laid his right hand on Bingzhang's shoulder. "It's been nearly twenty years. Why haven't we heard anything from her since then?"

"Opera has fallen on hard times in recent years," Bingzhang explained primly. "Xiao Yanqiu now spends most of her time teaching."

"Hard times?" The factory boss stiffened. "By that I take it you mean money." Thrusting his prominent chin in Bingzhang's direction, he said, "Let her sing."

Puzzled by this comment, Bingzhang tentatively

sounded the man out: "Does that mean you're offering to pay for a performance?"

The factory boss's arrogance resurfaced. "Let her sing," he repeated in the voice and countenance of a great man.

Qiao Bingzhang asked the waitress for a cup of *baijiu*. He rose from the table. "You aren't trying to be funny, are you?"

"The one thing we have at our factory is a bit of money," the man said, still arrogantly, but with the serious tone of someone making a formal report. "Don't presume that all we know how to do is fill our coffers and endanger the people's health. We also strive to promote a climate of culture."

The man remained seated, while Qiao Bingzhang stood, bent slightly at the waist. They clinked glasses, then Bingzhang tipped his head back and emptied the contents of his glass. On occasions when he was excited, as he was now, he tended to blur the line between honesty and flattery. "Today I am in the company of a *bodhisattva*," he said, "a true *bodhisattva*."

The Moon Opera, long a painful memory for the troupe, had been commissioned in 1958 as a political assignment. The troupe had planned to perform it in Beijing a year later as part of the fes-

3

tivities marking the Republic's tenth anniversary. But before the first performance could be staged, a certain general was unhappy with what he saw at rehearsal. "Our lands are lovely beyond description," he had said. "Why would any of our young maidens want to flee to the moon?" It was a simple comment but one that raised goose bumps on the troupe leader's flesh. *The Moon Opera* closed before it had opened.

Xiao Yanqiu's voice, it's fair to say, made *The Moon Opera* a hit, but one could also say that Xiao Yanqiu's star rose thanks to *The Moon Opera*. The opera's good fortunes ignited those of the performer, and the performer's fortunes sparked those of the opera, as is so often the case. But that was in 1979, when Xiao Yanqiu was nineteen. People pegged her as an emerging star, even at nineteen a natural for the role of a heartbroken woman. Everything about her — her eyes, her interpretation, her enunciation, and the way she tossed the water sleeves of her costume — was imbued with an inbred aura of tragedy: sad, melancholy, and fanciful. At the age of fifteen she had appeared on the stage as Li Tiemei in the revolutionary model opera *The Red Lantern.* Holding her lantern high as she stood beside Granny Li, she had evoked no sense of incorruptibility, no thundering spirit of "never leave the battlefield until all the jackals are dead!" Instead, like autumn winds and rain, she'd left her audience with feelings of intense melancholy, so angering the old troupe leader that he shouted at the director, "Where did you get that little seductress?"

It was in 1979 that *The Moon Opera* had a second chance; this time it was staged. During the dress rehearsal, everyone fell silent the moment Xiao Yanqiu began to sing. And as he watched her up on the stage, the old troupe leader, who had only recently taken up his post again, muttered, "That girl knows the taste of bitter gall. She was born to wear water sleeves."

A one-time entertainer who had studied at an old opera school, the old troupe leader had been a man whose word carried considerable weight. And so nineteen-year-old Xiao Yanqiu was elevated to be principal portrayer of Chang'e. Her understudy was none other than the renowned portrayer of maiden roles, Li Xuefen. In a performance of the model opera *Azalea Mountain* years earlier, Li had excelled in the role of the heroine Ke Xiang, and had then enjoyed a spell of popularity. Now that she was relegated to the status of understudy, she displayed the magnanimity befitting a once-success-ful performer. At the cast meeting she rose to say, "For the future of the troupe, I shall be happy to de-vote myself to the training of others, to selflessly make my experience on the stage available to Com-rade Xiao Yanqiu, and to pass the baton in a worthy manner." Her eyes brimming with tears, Xiao Yan-qiu joined the others in a hearty round of applause.

Yes, Xiao Yanqiu's voice made *The Moon Opera* a hit. The cast staged performances throughout the prov-ince, and they were the talk of the town wherever they went. Older aficionados reflected on past per-formances, while younger members of the audi-ence marveled at the classical costumes. Provincial cultural circles welcomed this "second spring-time," as they did "all other battlefronts." *The Moon Opera* was all the rage, which, naturally, flung the contemporary Chang'e, Xiao Yanqiu, into the pub-lic eye. A famous general from the military com-mand, known for his talents as a calligrapher, praised her performance effusively. In the style of a great poem by Marshal Ye Jianying, he wrote: *Fearlessly besiege a city wall / Courageously stage a difficult play / The drama troupe may find it a tough call / But hard work will see you through the day.* That was followed by the inscription: "For Young Comrade Yanqiu, in mutual encouragement." He then invited her to his home and, after reminiscing about the good old days, presented her with the framed poem in his own calligraphy, which she could hang on a wall.

Who could have predicted that "Young Comrade Yanqiu" would one day wreck her own career? After the incident, an old-time entertainer was heard to say that they should never have staged *The Moon Opera*. Each person has her own destiny; so do operas. *The Moon Opera* was too feminine, contained far too much *yin*. If they insisted on staging it, they should have balanced the roles with a male singing character. And Houyi the Archer ought to have been played by a "Brass Hammer," a *Hualian*, not a *Laosheng*, even if that had meant getting one on loan from another troupe. If they'd done that, they could have avoided the troubles that ensued, and Xiao Yanqiu would not have done what she did.

IT WAS A WORLD of snow and ice on the day a special performance of *The Moon Opera* was staged for the Armored Division as an expression of gratitude to the troops. Li Xuefen asked to be given the role that day, a reasonable request, when you consider it. She was, after all, the designated understudy.

Xiao Yanqiu, on the other hand, was decidedly un-reasonable, and she hogged the role from the be-ginning, not once letting her understudy go on stage. The Chang'e role was a demanding one, with many arias, and Xiao Yanqiu was fond of saying: "I'm young," "For me it's not a problem," "The maiden role requires no acrobatics," and "I can manage easily." Truth is, most people had no doubt that, for all her purported reticence, Yanqiu had high ambitions and no intention of sharing the banquet with anyone. Clinging to a growing desire for fame and fortune, she was intent on placing herself ahead of Li Xuefen.

There was no way of reasoning with her, and when the leadership summoned her, her lovely face turned pork-liver purple. They relented by as-signing Xuefen the job of "offering the youngster some guidance and advice," of "giving her a bit of support." But this time Li Xuefen would not budge. When she starred in *Azalea Mountain*, she said, they had often staged the opera at military bar-racks, and, earlier that afternoon, several of the soldiers had spotted her and called out "Ke Xiang." As the bedrock of her support, the soldiers would not let anyone else take the stage.

Li Xuefen won over the officers and men of

the Armored Division, who saw in her portrayal of Chang'e an echo of the commanding presence of Ke Xiang — PLA cap, straw sandals, and pistol in hand — even though on this night Ke Xiang was in traditional costume. Li Xuefen had a booming voice with a crisp, clear tone, one that bespoke passion. Her sonority had evolved and strengthened over a decade or more, until it was widely recognized and dubbed the "Li Xuefen school of operatic singing." On that basis, she had created a series of heroic women: audiences watched as women warriors fought to the death, they witnessed the valor of female soldiers, they were moved by the lofty sentiments of urban women in the countryside, and they marveled at the sight of female branch secretaries. The emphasis of Li's performance that night was on the resonant quality of her voice, and the soldiers rewarded her with applause that was both rhythmic and loud, reminiscent of the marching cadence of a military review. No one so much as noticed Xiao Yanqiu, who had appeared halfway through the opera, an army greatcoat draped over her shoulders as she stood aloof in the wings to watch Li Xuefen's performance. Disaster had already begun to settle around Xiao Yanqiu; it was descending on Li Xuefen too.

The Moon Opera was over. After five curtain calls, Li Xuefen went backstage, trying, but not quite succeeding, to mask her self-satisfaction. There she ran into Xiao Yanqiu; they faced one another, heated excitement rising from one, cold emanating from the other. When Xuefen saw the look on Yanqiu's face, she went up to greet her, taking both of Yanqiu's hands in hers. "Were you watching, Yanqiu?" she asked.

"Yes."

"Was it all right?"

Xiao Yanqiu held her tongue.

Others had come up and encircled them.

Li Xuefen shrugged off her army greatcoat and said, "Yanqiu, there's something I've been meaning to talk to you about. See what you think of this, like this, if we sing the line this way, it's more moving, don't you think? Ah, like this." She curled her fingers, petal-like, arched her eyebrows, and began to sing. Now, entertainers all know that professional rivals are bitter foes, even if one is a master teaching an apprentice. "A teacher would rather teach voice than lyrics, and rather teach lyrics than mood." But not Li Xuefen. She had taught Xiao Yanqiu everything there was to know about the Li school of operatic singing.

Yanqiu stared at Xuefen and said nothing.

The others stood around, observing the troupe's two female leads, one high-minded and talented, the other humble and studious, and they sighed with a palpable sense of relief. But a troubling look clouded Xiao Yanqiu's face, one of disdain. Everyone knew how arrogant the girl was, but now not only did she not *feel* humble, she did not *look* it.

Li Xuefen was oblivious.

Following her demonstration, she again sought Xiao Yanqiu's opinion. "That way you see a laboring woman from the old society. Doing it this way is better, wouldn't you say?"

Xiao Yanqiu just stared at Li Xuefen, an odd look on her face. "Not bad," she said with the hint of a smile before Xuefen could continue. "But you forgot two props today."

Li Xuefen clasped her hands to her chest, and from there to her head. "What did I forget?" she asked anxiously.

Xiao Yanqiu took her time to reply. "A pair of straw sandals and a pistol," she said at last.

At first everyone was lost, but they, as well as Li Xuefen, soon realized what was happening. This time the upstart had gone too far. Just because she saw the world immodestly was no reason to speak that way. Still smiling, she gazed at Xuefen, watching her passion slowly cool.

"What about you? What kind of Chang'e are you? A bad luck woman, a seductress, a nymphomaniac! Imprisoned on the moon and unable to sell her goods!" Xuefen rose up on her toes, the heat of passion returning.

Now it was Xiao Yanqiu's turn to cool off. A north wind blew from her nostrils, and snowflakes swirled in her eyes, as if she had been struck by something. A stagehand walked up with a mug of hot water for Li Xuefen to warm her hands. Xiao Yanqiu reached out, took the mug from him, and flung the water in Li Xuefen's face.

BACKSTAGE WAS suddenly a hornets' nest. Xiao Yanqiu stood watching with a dazed look as figures darted back and forth, her ears assailed by the chaotic clatter of footsteps. Feet pounded the floor, running from backstage to the hallway, and from there to somewhere outside, where footfalls were replaced by the starting of a car engine. Then she was alone, the abandoned hallway a road to the moon, it seemed. After standing there bewildered for a long moment, she walked down the lonely hallway to her dressing room, where she stood in front of the mirror and, with a startled look, stared at her reflection. Only now did she comprehend what she had done. Gazing absently at her hands, she sat down on the dressing-room stool.

Just how hot the water had been no longer mattered. As always, the nature of the act determined the degree of its severity. Xiao Yanqiu's stalwart supporter, the old troupe leader, was so angry his head looked like it might explode. Wagging two fingers a scant few inches from Xiao Yanqiu's nose, he sputtered, "You, you, you, you you you you you, why you little!" Words failed him, and he was forced to revert to lines from the operatic repertoire: "You must not forsake your conscience. If fame and fortune cloud your heart, jealousy will bring you to grief."

"That's not what it was," Xiao Yanqiu said.

"Then what was it?"

"Not that," she said through her tears.

The old troupe leader pounded the table. "Then what was it?"

"I mean it. That's not what it was."

Xiao Yanqiu left the stage.

The principal portrayer of Chang'e was demoted to the position of a teacher in the drama academy; her understudy lay in a hospital ward. *The Moon Opera* closed for the second time. "Buds appear and die in a frost, plum blossoms fall before hailstones."

Fortune did not favor *The Moon Opera*.

T W O

WHO COULD HAVE predicted that *The
Moon Opera* would find a patron, its own
bodhisattva?

The costume money finally arrived.

Qiao Bingzhang had been weighted down with
worries, waiting for days. Without the tobacco factory money, *The Moon Opera* would be nothing more
than the moon in the water. Truth is, he had only
been waiting eleven days, but to him it seemed like
an eternity. As he was waiting, he discovered that
while the amount of money was important, so too
was how long it took to get there. These days that
thing called money was getting stranger all the
time.

At the preliminary troupe meeting Bingzhang
was surprised by the extent of opposition to Xiao
Yanqiu returning to the stage; they had reached an

impasse, unable to move beyond this single issue. He spun his ballpoint pen as he listened to the people around the table. Finally, he flipped the pen onto the table, leaned back in his chair, and, with a smile, said, "Ease off a bit, can't we? The man asked for her by name. There's nothing shameful in letting money call the shots these days." A heavy silence settled over the conference room. No one spoke, and while that could have been interpreted as a sign of opposition, at least it left room for compromise. Li Xuefen had left the troupe to open a hotel, which was fortunate, as her singing style was something Bingzhang could not have borne. The others held their tongue; they didn't say yes, they didn't say no. Sometimes, of course, silence means consent, so Bingzhang decided to test the waters: "I guess that's settled then," he mumbled vaguely.

But then the problematic issue of who would be the understudy surfaced. Being an understudy to a star was never considered desirable, but especially if that star was Xiao Yanqiu. It was left to old Gao to come up with a workable solution, which was to let Xiao Yanqiu choose her understudy from among her own students. No matter how jealous, how fixated she was on fame and fortune, she surely wouldn't fight over a role with her own students.

On this point there was agreement. But what old Gao said next threw Bingzhang into a state of anxiety. "I think we're wasting our breath," he said. "It's been twenty years, and Yanqiu is a forty-year-old woman. Could she still have the voice it takes? I, for one, doubt it."

Why didn't I think of that? Bingzhang reproached himself silently. Twenty years, that is how long it had been. Twenty years, and in that time even the best steel will rust through. Bingzhang muffled a sigh. The meeting had been going on for nearly two hours, all tied up with Xiao Yanqiu, and nothing had been resolved. A preparatory meeting. Anything but! More like a look back at the past. When they didn't have the money, money was all they thought about. Now that the money had arrived, no one knew how to spend it. There was more to this money than the length of time it had taken to get there, for it was inextricably linked to the past. Indeed, that thing called money was getting very strange.

Bingzhang needed to hear Xiao Yanqiu sing; otherwise, he might as well use the factory money to make firecrackers and at least get a few loud bangs out of it.

She came to the conference room at the appointed time and sat down, and he immediately realized he'd made a miscalculation; with just the two of them in an otherwise empty conference room, him at one end of a long, oval table and her at the other, it felt much too formal. She had put on weight, but was as frosty and aloof as ever, emitting coldness like an air conditioner. He'd intended to talk first about *The Moon Opera*, which for her, he belatedly recalled, was and always had been an open wound; now he had no idea what to say.

To some degree, Bingzhang was afraid of Xiao Yanqiu, although in point of fact he was a generation older than she. But her temper was justifiably famous. She could seem as formless as water, giving the impression that she would meekly submit to oppression and abuse. But if you were careless enough to actually come up against her, she would turn frosty in the proverbial blink of an eye, and was capable of bringing things to a shattering conclusion through sudden and reckless actions. That is why the dining-hall workers at the drama school all said, "We chefs use salad oil whenever we cook, and we avoid Xiao Yanqiu by hook or by crook."

Not knowing how to broach the subject at hand, Bingzhang beat around the bush, one moment asking how things were going for her and the next asking about her teaching and students. He even brought up the weather. All of it meaningless chatter. After a few minutes, she spoke up. "What exactly did you want to talk to me about?"

Her bluntness so unnerved Bingzhang that he replied without thinking, "Let's hear a line or two."

Yanqiu gazed at him and rested her arms on the table to form a half circle, giving no hint of what was going through her mind at that moment. Then, with a stare devoid of expression, she asked him, "What do you want to hear? The *Xipi* tune of 'Flying to Heaven' or the *Erhuang* aria 'The Vast Cold Palace'?"

By offering the two most famous pieces in *The Moon Opera*, which had brought her two decades of misery, Yanqiu was being openly provocative, slamming a bullet into the chamber. Instinctively, Bingzhang straightened up and prepared for the verbal assault that was sure to come. Yet he wasn't too concerned. He also had a card to play. "Sing a bit of the *Erhuang.*"

Yanqiu stood up, moved away from her chair, tugged at the front of her jacket and smoothed the back; then she turned to look out the window, taking a moment to compose herself before her hands and eyes began to move and she drifted into the role. Her singing had the same depth of roots and breadth of canopy as ever, and Bingzhang was deprived of even a moment to be surprised, as unexpected joy flooded his heart and a greedy yet remorseful Chang'e materialized before him. With his eyes shut, he thrust his right hand into his pants pocket and curled his fingers to drum the beat: hard soft-soft-soft, hard soft-soft-soft.

Yanqiu sang straight through for fifteen minutes. When she finished, Bingzhang opened his eyes and squinted to size up the woman before him. The *Erhuang* piece she'd just sung had gone from slow and meandering to a lyrical rhythm, and then to a strong beat, leading to a crescendo, a complex and demanding melody that required a broad vocal range. She had been away from the stage for twenty years, yet sang it beautifully, without missing a note; clearly, she had never stopped practicing. Bingzhang sat sprawled in his chair, not moving yet deeply moved. Twenty years, he sighed to himself, it's been twenty years. A tangle of emotions filled his heart. "How did you manage to keep at it?"

"Keep at what?" she asked him. "What is it I'm supposed to have kept at?"

"It's been twenty years. It couldn't have been easy."

"I didn't *keep* at anything." Finally grasping what he was getting at, she looked up and said, "I *am* Chang'e."

Xiao Yanqiu emerged from Qiao Bingzhang's office in a daze. It was October, a windy but sunny day more like spring than autumn. The sunshine and the wind were bright and breezy, alluring and undulating, but it felt unreal, almost dreamlike, as they lingered by her side. She roamed the streets aimlessly, stepping on her own shadow. But then she stopped, looked around, distracted, and glanced down absentmindedly at her shadow, short and squat in the early afternoon sun, almost dwarf-like. It was virtually shapeless, like a puddle of water. She couldn't take her eyes off it. When she stepped forward, her shadow crawled ahead like a giant toad. Suddenly focused and clearheaded, Xiao Yanqiu was convinced that the shadow on the ground was her true self, while the upright body was merely an appendage to it. And so it is: people often achieve true awareness of who they really are in the midst of one lonely moment. Her eyes glazed over again; sorrow and despair had turned into an October wind coming at her from one indefinite location before drifting off to yet another.

She decided to go on a diet, starting now.

When fate unexpectedly smiles on her, a woman will often begin a new phase in her life by dieting. Xiao Yanqiu hailed a cab and went straight to People's Hospital, a place that still held heartbreaking memories for her. In all those years, she'd refused to see a doctor there even when her kidneys were causing her discomfort. People's Hospital had been the scene of a life-changing event; it was where her heart had been broken. On the second day of Li Xuefen's hospitalization, Xiao Yanqiu had been forced by the old troupe leader to go to the hospital, where Xuefen had made it clear that she would consider letting Xiao Yanqiu off the hook only if she was satisfied with her rival's attitude during her self-criticism. Everyone in the troupe knew that the old leader would do whatever was necessary to protect Xiao Yanqiu. He personally wrote a self-criticism for her to read at the hospital, telling her in no uncertain terms that she must perform well in front of Li Xuefen before anything else could be said or done. Yanqiu folded up the self-criticism after reading it, anxiety clouding her judgment. "I wasn't jealous," she defended herself, "and I never intended to ruin her looks." The old troupe leader felt like slapping her, as his eyes turned red from anger at her obstinacy, especially

22

at a moment like this. But he could not bring himself to hit this childish woman. With a sweep of his arm, he said, raising his voice, "I spent seven years in prison, and I have no desire to visit you there." As she stared at his receding back, she saw that a terrible future lay waiting for her somewhere up ahead.

In the end, she did go to People's Hospital, where Li Xuefen lay in a hospital bed, her face swathed in gauze. All the troupe's important people, including the creator of *The Moon Opera*, had crowded into the room. With her hands clasped low in front, Xiao Yanqiu walked up to Li Xuefen's bed, eyes downcast. Staring at her feet, she began by swearing, cursing everyone in her family, back some eight generations, reviling them as worse than shit. The room was deathly quiet when she'd finished; no one spoke a word or made a sound, except for Li Xuefen, who coughed dryly behind the gauze. The air in the room turned oppressive. What could anyone say? Xiao Yanqiu had to consider herself lucky that Li Xuefen had not filed a complaint at the Public Security station.

Unable to bear the stifling atmosphere, Yanqiu looked around with tear-filled eyes for someone to come to her aid. The old troupe leader stood in the doorway, glaring at her. Knowing she had no way out, she slowly removed the self-criticism from her pocket, unfolded it, one sheet at a time, and began to read. Like a typewriter key hitting the paper, she spat out one word after another. When she was done, everyone breathed a sigh of relief, for the contents of the self-criticism confirmed the offender's positive attitude. Li Xuefen pulled the gauze away from her face, exposing reddish purple splotches of skin shining under a coat of greasy ointment. She accepted the self-criticism and reached for Xiao Yanqiu's hands. "Yanqiu," she said with a smile, "you're still young, you must try to be more broad-minded. You have to change." Yanqiu managed to get a glimpse of her expression before Xuefen rewrapped her face. That smile was a glass filled with hot but not quite scalding water that splashed onto her heart; with a sizzle, it doused an inner flame.

Xiao Yanqiu emerged from the room into bright sunlight. She walked to the top of the stairs, stopped beside the handrail, and turned back in time to see the old troupe leader heave a sigh of relief. He nodded, and she responded with a smile that turned into a laugh. Then she lost it completely, letting out loud belly laughs, her shoulders rising and falling like a bearded clown laughing wildly on the opera stage. Everyone nearby heard this unusual racket and stuck their heads out of the wards to gape at Xiao Yanqiu. But she kept laughing, uncontrollably, until her knees buckled and she fell headlong to the landing between the fourth and third floors. People rushed to her side, where she lay on the concrete floor within earshot of the troupe leader, who explained to anyone who would listen, "Her attitude isn't bad. She still has a good attitude."

That was twenty years ago. Now, Xiao Yanqiu registered to see a doctor in the urology department. Once she had her prescription filled, she walked out behind the hospital. Twenty years. From a distance, she could see people entering and leaving the inpatient building. It had changed, with mosaic tiles on the exterior walls, but the roof, the windows, and the corridors still looked the same, so maybe it wasn't that different. Standing there, she realized that, contrary to what people say, life does not reach into the future; rather, it points to the past, at least in terms of its framework and structure.

She arrived home an hour later than usual and saw that her daughter was slouching over the dining-room table doing her homework. Her husband was slumped on the sofa, watching TV with the sound off. She leaned against the door frame, grasping her prescription bag from People's Hospital as she observed her husband with a sense of fatigue. He could tell that something was wrong, so he got up and walked over to her. She handed him the prescription, went to the bedroom, and shut the door behind her. He turned his gaze from her to the bag, from which he took out a box and examined it, filled with uncertainty. The printing was in a foreign language, indecipherable to him, which only worsened the situation.

With a sense of impending doom, he followed her into the bedroom. No sooner had he stepped through the door than she threw herself at him, wrapping her arms around his neck and pulling him to her until their bodies were crushed together, tighter and tighter. He knew at once that she was struggling to bear up under an assault of crippling sadness. The prescription fell from his hand. He stepped backward and banged the door, slamming it shut, and as he held her in his arms, destructive thoughts raced through his mind. Finally she cried out, "Miangua, I'm going back on the stage."

As if not comprehending what she had just said, he lifted her head to look more closely, a mixture of relief and doubt in his eyes. "I can be on the stage again," she said. Shoving her away, in a state of shock, he blurted out, "That's it? That's what this is all about?"

She stole an embarrassed look at him and smiled. "I feel sad, that's all," she muttered through an onset of tears.

He turned and opened the door to go warm up her dinner, only to discover their daughter stand-ing there timidly. Even his bones felt lighter, now that he had escaped the possibility of calamity, but he frowned and said roughly, "Go do your home-work!"

Xiao Yanqiu pulled her husband back into the room and waved to her daughter to come in and sit beside her so she could get a good look at her. Born with a large frame and a square face, she did not take after her mother; she was, in fact, a carbon copy of her father. But on this night, to Xiao Yanqiu her daughter seemed prettier than ever, and a more detailed examination revealed that the girl looked like her, after all, just one size bigger. Miangua turned to go into the kitchen, but Yanqiu said, "No need. I'm on a diet."

He stopped and stood in the doorway, puzzled. "What for? Have I complained that you're getting fat?"

Laying her hand on her daughter's head, Yanqiu said, "You may not care if I'm overweight, but no audience would ever accept a fat Chang'e."

Now when good fortune has smiled on a couple, the first order of business is to put the children to bed. Once the youngsters are asleep, the adults can head to their bed for the celebration ceremony. In this way a happy night is as quiet as water yet lights up like fireworks. The promise of unanticipated delights had Miangua running around the flat, busying himself in one room and another, not quite knowing what to do.

A traffic policeman who had served in the army, he was rough around the edges, insensitive, and devoid of tact. Where marriage was concerned, the best he had hoped for was to find a worker in a government-run factory. Never, not in his wildest dreams, had the possibility entered his head that a famed beauty, that Chang'e herself, would become his wife. That's what it had felt like, a dream.

The process had been old-fashioned, nothing new. A matchmaker had introduced them beside a willow tree in the park, and they had begun dating.

After doing this for a while, they hurried into the "bridal chamber."

Back in those days, Xiao Yanqiu had been an ice queen. On the cobblestone path in the park, she looked more like a sleepwalker, a zombie who had lost her soul, than an ordinary pedestrian. Yet rather than diminish a woman's beauty, that sort of look often makes her more alluring. For it enriches her with an ephemeral grace that makes a man's heart skip a beat and in turn instills in him a desire to love and protect her. When Miangua first laid eyes upon Yanqiu, his hands went cold, and the chill reached down to the pit of his stomach. She was shrouded in a frigid air, like a glass sculpture, and his immediate reaction was to feel unworthy. He silently cursed the matchmaker, for no matter how you looked at it, such a sparkling beauty was way out of his league. He walked gingerly down the cobblestone path with her, not daring to speak because she was so quiet. For him the early days of their relationship were not so much dating as unimaginable torture. But the torment was mixed with an indescribable sweetness. She remained cold and stern, her eyes unfocused, as if her soul had truly left her. At first he thought she didn't care for him, but she always arrived on time, though looking unwell, when he asked her to go for a walk. Clearly, he had known nothing of her state of mind, for in fact she was possessed by the desire to marry herself off, the sooner the better. As inept at dating as he was, she walked with him, never saying a word. In her presence, Miangua's self-esteem was in tatters, and he hadn't an ounce of imagination. The park's path was where they had met, so that was invariably where their dates could and, in fact, must take place. Focused on her singular goal, she never asked him anything, and was a shadow that went where he went, which was the same place day after day; he didn't know where else to go. They walked down the same path, headed in the same direction, turned and rested at the same spots. Then they parted at the same place, where he would say the same thing, settling on a day and time for their next meeting.

But one day everything changed — by accident, of course. That day she tripped and fell. She had been gazing at the moon and the heel of her shoe caught in a crack between cobblestones, turning her ankle and sending her tumbling to the ground. Miangua was so horrified his face turned whiter than the moon. Slow by nature, he was a man who could saunter along even if his head were on fire.

But not this time; this time he was scared witless, so flustered he didn't know what to do. Finally, he picked her up and carried her to the hospital; then, in the same flustered state, he took her home. Her ankle was swollen, black and blue, and she had skinned her elbow.

Unlike Miangua, Xiao Yanqiu was unconcerned about her injuries, almost as if she'd seen someone else fall and get hurt. That lack of concern gave the impression that if someone were to cut off her head and place it on a table, she'd still be composed, calmly blinking her eyes.

Miangua was the one who felt the pain. It hurt him to see her like that, and he stared at her ankle, not daring to look her in the eye. Eventually, he glanced at her, but quickly looked away. "Does it still hurt?" he asked in a tiny voice barely loud enough for her to hear. At that moment, she was not so much a glass sculpture, but a block of ice. Her glacial demeanor remained unchanged, as if she had become petrified. What she could not tolerate, not now, not here, was warmth. Even the lingering warmth from someone's hand would be enough to crumble her exterior and make her melt away.

Rather woodenly, he said in a pained voice,

"Let's not go out again. See how it made you fall and hurt yourself." She stared at him, while he reproached himself foolishly. If chiding himself in that jumbled, clumsy way of his wasn't a sign of concern and tenderness, what was it? Yanqiu felt a surge of emotion, and all past hurts and injuries came rushing back to her. Drop by drop, the ice began to melt, dripping away faster and faster. It was too late to stop the process; she was losing control and could not recapture her coldness. She clasped Miangua's hands and wanted to say his name, but couldn't, for she had begun to wail. She howled at the top of her lungs, shamefully loud, but didn't care. Miangua, on the other hand, was so perplexed he felt like bolting; but he couldn't, for she was holding on to him for dear life. He could not and did not get away.

Neither Yanqiu nor Miangua realized the significance of her momentous wails. There are times when a woman seems to have been born to belong to the person for whom she cries.

So Xiao Yanqiu, a teacher at the drama academy, hastily married herself off. She was adrift in a vast ocean, and Miangua was her lifeboat. For her, this union was her only chance; there would be no future prospects. What pleased her about Miangua was that he was a man with whom one could live a normal life; he cared about family and was steady, considerate, hardworking, even a tiny bit selfish. What else could she ask for? Hadn't she wanted a man with whom she could spend the rest of her life? He had one flaw though: he was greedy in bed, like a ravenous child who refuses to leave the table until he can no longer straighten up from all the food. But was that really a flaw? What she found puzzling was how a man could derive so much enjoyment from the same few jerky motions every time. He wore himself out, as if engaged in hard work. But he loved her, and one night, after he had finished, he said absurdly, "If we never have a daughter, you'll be my daughter." She pondered his preposterous comment for a week. While she wasn't particularly fond of lovemaking, she could still recall times when she actually enjoyed it.

Yanqiu was the one who ordered their daughter to bed that night, and from the way she let her lashes droop, Miangua could guess that the night would end with a splendid finale. In all their years of marriage, he had always had to beg for sex. This was a new experience. She stood by their daughter's bedroom and called out softly. Hearing no response, Miangua, who had stayed in the living

33

room, rubbed his hands expectantly. Yanqiu went into the bedroom, undressed in silence before slipping under the covers, then reached out an arm and laid it on top of the bedding.

"Miangua," she said, "come here."

Xiao Yanqiu was a wanton woman that night, determined to please him, catering to his every whim. Like a leaf in a summer windstorm, she opened up and laid herself out, rolling and rocking in wild abandon. She talked the whole time, and some of what she said was quite racy; she had to keep her voice low, but every word sizzled. Panting hard, she pleaded with him, her lips touching his ear. "I feel like screaming, Miangua," she said in a pained voice. "I feel like screaming!" She was a different person, a total stranger, and to him this augured the beginning of the good life. He could not have been happier; lost in pleasure, he forgot everything else. That night, he went crazy; she went even crazier.

THREE

AFTER CAREFUL CALCULATION, Bingzhang decided to host a banquet for the
tobacco-factory boss with money from
the costume funds. A memorable dinner would not
be cheap, but perhaps he could recoup some of that
money from the factory. For now, it was essential to
please the big man, for only if he was happy would
the troupe be happy. In the past, all Bingzhang had
needed to care about was making sure the leadership was happy; now that wasn't enough. As the
troupe leader, he had to scratch the backs of the
leadership *and* the factory manager, and he needed
to do well on both counts. Things began to fall into
place once he sent invitations to the factory manager and several high-ranking guests, plus a few
reporters. The more people, the livelier the event.
So long as he had a full plate of fine ingredients, he

could toss everything, meat and vegetables, into the proverbial hot pot. Didn't Chairman Mao say that revolution is not a dinner party? True enough. But Bingzhang wasn't remotely interested in starting a revolution; all he wanted was to take care of business. And that's what a banquet does: it takes care of business.

Naturally, the factory manager was the guest of honor; people like that are born to be the center of attention. Bingzhang spent the night beaming, smiling so much he had to take an occasional bathroom break to massage his cheeks so his smile wouldn't look stiff or forced. Fake goods were be-ing sold everywhere these days, and since this event was so important to him, Bingzhang's smile and expressions also had to be faked.

He had hoped that once he got his hands on the costume money, he could relax a bit. But no, he was more nervous, more anxious than ever. It had been years since the troupe had put on a performance, time that had passed with nothing to show for it. A drama troupe differs from an association of artists or writers, whose members, though perhaps old and alone at home, can collect a salary just by keeping their arms and legs moving: designing a few signs, painting some winter plums or bunches of grapes, or attacking someone in the evening paper. In a word, their value can increase with age. A drama troupe is nothing like that. No matter how good they are, opera performers cannot stay home and put on a play. Of course, in order to get a good housing assignment or a promotion, outside of sucking up to troupe leaders, the good ones must play all the roles — the *Sheng, Dan, Jing, Mo,* and *Chou.* Peking Opera is like no other art form. Whether they are speaking, singing, reading, tumbling, or playing an instrument, though they are touted as "artists," the performers rely on the strength of their bodies; it is how they make their living. Their bodies are worn out by the time they reach a certain age, and then they are like a desert — pour water on sand, and it disappears without a sizzle. Not only do they bring in no revenue, but they require double the investment, unlike a seasoned warrior, who is the equal of two men.

Bingzhang worried about money all the time. As he saw it, in addition to being in charge of a drama troupe, he was well on his way to becoming a merchant, waiting for the capital to roll in. He was reminded of a phrase he'd heard at a political study group, one made famous by a high-ranking official:

capital came into the world dripping blood and filth from head to toe. How true. Capital does drip blood; whether it's filthy or not is a topic for another day. The troupe was waiting for that blood to drip, counting on it to produce and produce more, and expand to produce even more. Its life was on the line. Bingzhang couldn't wait for *The Moon Opera* to be staged; the sooner the better. The longer the night, the more the dreams; things happen. Money's the key, only money.

The banquet reached its climactic moment when the factory boss met Xiao Yanqiu, which is to say, the banquet was one long climactic moment. Before the food was served, Bingzhang led Yanqiu into the room ceremoniously and, with the same degree of formality, introduced her to the guest of honor. For him, the meeting was a social event, perhaps even entertainment, but for Xiao Yanqiu it was a critical moment in her life; it would determine what the second half of that life would be like. When first notified of the banquet, rather than being overjoyed, she had been overwhelmed by enormous dread, immediately reminded of the famous *Qingyi* of an earlier generation, Li Xuefen's teacher, Liu Ruobing. Liu, who had been the most famous beauty on the 1950s stage, was also the first

38

celebrated actress to fall when the Cultural Revolution was launched.

The story of Liu's life up to the day of her death was well known in the drama troupe. In 1971, an aficionado who had risen to the position of deputy army commander took it upon himself to find out what had happened to his opera idol. He had his guards crawl under a stage and drag Liu Ruobing out. She was demonically ugly, with dried excrement and menstrual blood caked on her pant legs. The deputy commander stood off to the side, took one look, and climbed back into his military Jeep, leaving behind a line for the ages: "One must not soil oneself just to sleep with a famous person."

With Bingzhang's invitation in hand, Xiao Yanqiu's thoughts were of Liu Ruobing, although she could not say why. She spent half of her monthly wages in a beauty shop, where she sat in front of a full-length mirror to be made up as attractively as possible. The beautician's fingers were soft, but they hurt. To Xiao Yanqiu, this was less a beauty treatment than self-inflicted torture. Men fight other men, but women spend their whole lives fighting themselves.

The factory manager did not put on any airs, and was actually humble in Xiao Yanqiu's presence.

Calling her "Teacher," he politely and repeatedly invited her to take the seat of honor. Dismissive of the Cultural Bureau directors at the banquet, he had the highest regard for art and for artists. Essentially hijacked, Yanqiu was forced to sit between the Bureau Chief and the factory manager, directly across from her troupe leader. Sandwiched between luminaries who would determine her fate, she was justifiably nervous. Remaining faithful to her diet, she ate little, which made her seem intimidated by her surroundings, lacking the mannerisms appropriate for an actress who, twenty years before, had been the top *Qingyi*. Luckily for her, the guest of honor did not seem to want her to say much, for he talked the whole time. He spoke quietly but animatedly about the past, and said that he was a great admirer of "Teacher" Xiao Yanqiu and had been a die-hard fan back then. Smiling politely, she twisted the hair behind her ear with her pinkie, a sure sign of modesty and humility. Then he began to describe performances of *The Moon Opera*, telling her that back when he was still living in the countryside, an idle, bored young man, he had followed the troupe as it made the rounds throughout the province. He even recounted an anecdote: Once, when Xiao Yanqiu was suffering from a cold, she coughed during her third performance. Rather than boo, the audience showered her with applause. The banquet table went quiet. The factory boss turned to her and said, "I was part of that." Everyone laughed and clapped, including the factory manager himself. The applause was joyful and rallying, an implication that there was more to come, and that it was a pity they hadn't met earlier, but that it was wonderful they were sharing a good time now. They raised their glasses in a toast.

The factory manager talked on, in a confidential tone, about a broad range of issues, including international affairs, the WTO, Kosovo, Chechnya, Hong Kong, Macao, reforms and liberalization, the future and its obstacles, the marketing and production of drama, and people's popular tastes. He was good. The guests nodded and reflected somberly, as if these were things that had been on their minds all along, an important part of their daily life, like cooking oil, salt, soy sauce, and vinegar, and as if they had been racking their brains over these very things, but finding no solutions. And now, at last, the water had receded and the riverbed stones were exposed, all highways led to heaven, answers had been found and solutions formed. They downed another cup, experiencing relief for the future of humanity, for the nation, and for drama.

Bingzhang had been watching the factory manager all night. While grateful for what the man was doing, from their first meeting he had harbored a measure of disdain toward him. Now all that had changed. He was seeing the man in a different light, for not only was he a successful entrepreneur, he was also a sophisticated thinker and diplomat. In wartime, he might well have been a top military strategist and field commander. In a word, a great man. Obviously affected by the man's talk, Bingzhang said illogically, "You've got my vote when the People's Congress selects our next mayor!" The manager did not respond; lighting a cigarette, he made an ambiguous gesture and turned the dinner-table conversation back to Xiao Yanqiu.

He was clever, witty, and creative, especially when Xiao Yanqiu was the topic. They were about the same age, but he seemed so much older and wiser, a man who infused his concern, respect, and affection with the airs of a revered elder. Yet, he was also full of energy, and his masculine, worldly manner of placing himself on equal footing with the common people made him seem even more personable, and thus more her equal. Feeling like a woman caressed by a spring breeze, Yanqiu grew increasingly confident and more relaxed. Then once she began to feel at ease with herself, she engaged the guest of honor in conversation, and before long, his forehead glowed and his eyes lit up. Never taking them off her, he began talking faster, all the while accepting toasts from other guests. Not once since the banquet began had he stopped drinking; he accepted every toast, and by then had probably downed a quart of hard liquor. Oblivious of others around them, he talked exclusively with Yanqiu.

Bingzhang found all this drinking worrisome, given his familiarity with successful banquets that had been wrecked by a few too many glasses of liquor or a few too many words from a pretty woman. He was hoping his guest knew his limit. How many times had he witnessed a successful, even dignified man cross the line, thanks to alcohol, with a beautiful actress? He was concerned that his guest might say something inappropriate, or actually do something rash, and was worried sick, knowing that many great men had erred in the final phase of an event, for which they then paid a high price. Increasingly fearful that the banquet would not end well for his guest, Bingzhang made a show of checking the time on his wristwatch. But the factory manager turned a blind eye to this ploy and took out a cigarette, which he offered to Yanqiu, an unseemly action by almost anyone's standard.

Bingzhang gulped, certain that his guest was losing control. So, with his eyes fixed on the wineglass in front of him, he nervously sought a way to end the affair, one that would send his guest home feeling good about the experience, but that would also allow Xiao Yanqiu to come away in one piece. Apparently, his thoughts were transparent, even to Yanqiu, who smiled and said, "I don't smoke." The man nodded and lit it for himself. "Too bad. I was hoping you'd do an ad for me, featuring you on the moon." The guests were momentarily confused, but were quick to laugh, even though his comment wasn't particularly funny. Sometimes nonsense spouted by a great man can pass for humor.

They were still laughing when the factory manager stood up and said, "I had a wonderful time tonight," thus bringing the festivities to an end. He then signaled to his driver. "It's getting late," he said. "Drive Miss Xiao home." This came as a surprise. Bingzhang had been worried that the man would try to get something going with Xiao Yanqiu. But he didn't. In fact, he had conducted himself with such decorum and conversed with such care-free politeness that one might have thought he hadn't so much as touched his glass, as if the quart or so of hard liquor had been poured not down his gullet but into his pants pocket. Obviously a master banquet-goer, he was blessed with an admirable capacity for alcohol and a keen sense of when to stop. Bingzhang had put on a good show, supplying plates of phoenix head, pork belly, and leopard tail, the alpha to omega of any successful banquet.

But poor Xiao Yanqiu, caught unprepared for such a speedy end to the meal, found herself tongue-tied. Finally, she sputtered, "I've got my bike."

"A great artist cannot be made to ride a bike," the factory manager replied as he gestured for his driver to escort her to the car. Left with no good op-tion, and with a final glance at her dinner partner, Yanqiu fell in behind the driver. As she neared the door, she sensed that all eyes were on her; with rapt concentration on each step, and feeling hopelessly awkward, she nearly forgot how to walk. But no one could tell. They just stared at her back, her value having shot up a hundredfold. The woman now had herself a powerful backer.

The guest of honor turned to chat briefly with the Bureau Chief, inviting him to visit his factory. "You're quite the drinker!" Bingzhang cut in. "Like a sponge!" He repeated himself four or five times. Now why in the world had he tried to suck up to the man that way? He sounded either like a man with a complex or one who'd been given quite a scare. There was no response from the factory manager, who just smiled and, as he stubbed out his cigarette, changed the subject yet again.

FOUR

THERE IS TRUTH in the saying that good fortune will find a way into your house even if you shut the door. But good fortune seemed to have lost its mystique. Now it was all about money; only money could slip in through a crack in the doorway. What, after all, was so special about a cigarette-factory boss? Nowadays, there were more "bosses" on the street than swallows in the spring, than grasshoppers in the fall, than mosquitoes in the summer, or than snowflakes in the winter. This one had money, and since it wasn't his own, he made it readily available.

Meanwhile, the people in the drama troupe and those at the academy envied not Xiao Yanqiu, but the girl, Chunlai, who had stumbled into great good fortune.

Chunlai, who entered the academy at the age of

47

eleven, had studied under Xiao Yanqiu from grades two through seven. Anyone who knew Yanqiu also knew that Chunlai was more than just her student; she was like a daughter. When she started out, Chunlai had studied for the *Huadan* role — bold, seductive women — not *Qingyi* — chaste women and faithful wives. It was Xiao Yanqiu who brazenly took her over. *Qingyi* and *Huadan* are very different female roles, but with fewer opera fans these days, the two had been lumped together as *Huadan*. The confusion was caused in part by a lack of sophistication and knowledge on the part of the audience, but the prime culprit had been modern opera's greatest performer, Mei Lanfang. Mei had a vast and profound knowledge of Peking Opera, and over the course of his lengthy career blended the singing styles and acting formulae of the two female roles to create a new role, called *Huashan*. The emergence of *Huashan* embodied Mei's desire for innovation and creativity, but wound up creating unnecessary problems for later generations, who were far less concerned about any distinction between the two roles. To cite but one example, the so-called "four famous female leads" was an unfortunate general term, the true description for which should have been "two famous *Huadan* and two renowned *Qingyi*." All forms of drama were in decline, so almost no one cared if people could tell a *Qingyi* from a *Huadan*. But for those who studied or performed opera, the distinction had to be maintained. *Qingyi* was still *Qingyi*; *Huadan* remained *Huadan*. The differences in singing style, oral narration, costume, stage movements, and performance formulae were legion, like flowers on separate branches, each with its distinct bloom, but which never come together.

Chunlai had her reasons for wanting to study *Huadan*. A *Huadan* recites her lines in loud, crisp Beijing Mandarin, while a *Qingyi* drags out each word. Without translation or subtitles, it is harder to understand a *Qingyi* than to watch a pirated DVD. In short, a *Qingyi* speaks a language unknown to man. The differences are even more pronounced in terms of singing. A *Huadan* sings in a nimble, bright, clear manner, sounding a bit like a pop singer, with a pinched falsetto. Lively and fetching, she cocks her head as she leaps around like a chirpy sparrow. A *Qingyi*, on the other hand, takes forever to sing a single word, squeaking and creaking, swaying three times with each step, with one hand over her midsection and the other gesturing with a curved pinkie as she hums and croons; you could get up, go to the bathroom, finish your business, wipe yourself front and back, and return to your seat, only to find that she is still on the same word. With the decline of Peking Opera, the only true fans of the *Qingyi* were older, retired officials. Some of the renowned *Qingyi* performers had left the stage and changed into shiny black leather jackets to roar like lions in front of a microphone, their hair a fright, or signed up for TV soaps, where they played one man's concubine or another man's cutie. Either way, they received a bit of "cultural" coverage in the evening newspapers. No, a *Qingyi* could never be compared with a *Huadan*. There were so many variety shows on TV, and comics and pop singers could create as much racket as they wanted, but the national culture had to be actively promoted and the country's heritage needed to be maintained somehow. So, as they say, after singing "love the beauty more than national sovereignty," one at least must add "never leave the battlefield until all the jackals are dead." In the end, the *Huadan* provided a better future than the *Qingyi*, which may be why people jokingly referred to a drama troupe as an "Egg (Dan) nest."

In the second semester of her third year, Chunlai switched to the *Qingyi* role. She bore no resemblance to Xiao Yanqiu in her speaking voice, but when she sang, she was an echo of her mentor. The other teachers quipped that Chunlai was born to be Xiao Yanqiu's rival. When Yanqiu first tried to talk Chunlai into switching from *Huadan* to *Qingyi*, the girl had said no. Yanqiu kept working on her, but she wouldn't budge. Finally, not knowing what else to do, Xiao Yanqiu uttered a phrase that became and remains a source of amusement at the academy. She pulled a long face and said to Chunlai, "If you won't study at my knee, then I'll get down on my knee and beg. What do you say?" What could Chunlai say, when her teacher did something like that?

The people at the academy still recalled how Chunlai looked when she first arrived. She spoke with a heavy country accent and dressed in clothes with ridiculously short sleeves and cuffs, leaving her calves exposed above her socks. Her cheeks pruned up each winter, with red creases lining her face; no one would have believed that she would grow up to be such a beauty. She was a perfect example of the common wisdom that a girl changes dramatically at eighteen. Who could have predicted that such a rare opportunity would come to Xiao Yanqiu? And who would have thought that Chunlai would be so lucky as to be part of it?

In her twenty years at the academy Xiao Yanqiu had taught legions of students, but there hadn't been a true singer among them, not one who might carry on the tradition, let alone become famous. Considering herself to be a failure as a teacher, she nearly gave up. But not quite. Of the many kinds of pain one can suffer, the worst is being forced to face unpleasant realities. And that is what Xiao Yanqiu had to do. On her thirtieth birthday, she knew she was as good as dead. Then, over the next ten years, she sat at her mirror watching herself grow older day by day, witnessing the slow death of the celebrated Chang'e. And there wasn't a thing she could do about it. Her anxieties actually sped up the aging process; she could not hold off death with her hands nor claw it back with her fingernails.

Time is cruel to a woman. It is merciless and relentless. Thirty years old! Dear Father! Dear Mother! On her thirtieth birthday, she had her first taste of liquor. It was only a small cup, but enough for her to get truly drunk. She cut her kitchen apron into two pieces and, holding one in each hand and pretending they were the long, loose water sleeves of the opera costume, she waved the white, greasy cloth and stumbled around the kitchen, sending bottles of cooking oil, soy sauce, and vinegar crashing to the floor; a shard of broken glass cut her hand and stained the makeshift sleeves with drops of fresh red blood. The red and white water sleeves were flung into the air, then floated down, again and again. Miangua ran into the kitchen and grabbed her, but she looked at him vacantly and called him "My dear Mama." She recited the line to him in perfect pitch and tone: "My — dear — Ma — ma!" Seeing she was drunk, and fearful that her shouts would be heard, he covered her mouth with the blood-spattered apron. Yanqiu breathed deeply, her diaphragm rising and falling as she expelled the muffled roars of a wild animal. His heart ached to see her like this and he called her name, over and over. Though she turned her head to look at him, she could not speak. Yet the words emerged from her diaphragm, he could see that. She was calling from her diaphragm: "My — dear — Ma — ma — a — a!"

"A thousand *Sheng*, ten thousand *Dan*, but a good *Jing* is hard to find." So goes an old, but inaccurate saying passed down by performers from days long gone — one that found no support from

Xiao Yanqiu. Granted, it is almost impossible to find a *Hualian* among all the *Sheng, Dan, Jing,* and *Chou* roles, but there certainly aren't thousands of performers in any one category. From earliest days, *Qingyi* performers may well have numbered in the thousands, but a mere handful understood the role well enough to grasp its true essence. To be sure, a *Qingyi* must have a superb voice and an outstanding figure, but in the end, what makes an exceptional *Qingyi* is the type of woman who takes on the role, not how she sings or how she looks. Anyone born to play the role of a *Qingyi*, even a man six feet tall, must abandon the idea that his bones are made of clay and start acting as if his body were made of water. No matter which pier you drift to, you are still a cloud formed by water. On the stage, the *Qingyi* is not a succession of female roles, is not, in fact, even a gendered role. It is, in essence, an abstract concept, a profound form, an approach, a method, a significant natural gift. In a way, a person does not grow into being that woman, for she is not a product of the passage of time, nor can she be characterized by marriage or the biological stages of childbirth and nursing. A woman is just that, a woman. She cannot be learned nor can she be purged from a body. *Qingyi* is, one can almost say, a woman in name only; or, better yet, *Qingyi* is a woman among women, the ultimate woman, and a touchstone for all others. She appears on the stage, where she sings, signals with her eyes, and gestures with her hands — all components of so-called "performing" or "acting," yet never more than simple movements from daily life. She makes you feel that life is just like this — every woman walks like this and talks like this. If you are not that essential "woman," even if you were sitting on a sofa at home or perched at the head of your bed, you would be a bad performer, because you would be "acting," and the more you acted, the less you would look like "her." *Hualian*, the male painted-face role, is the exact parallel to the *Qingyi*. *Hualian* is the quintessential man; or, we might say, the quintessential profile of the quintessential man. Everything about man should be simple; body and soul are but a mask. So simple it is an exaggeration, so simple it is endless and changeless. Hence, the decline of Peking Opera began with the decline of man and woman, hand in hand; it was the degeneration of the sexes.

It was not easy for the gods to create a *Hualian*,

and just as hard for them to create a *Qingyi*. Xiao Yanqiu was one of the *Qingyi* rarities; Chunlai was another.

Xiao Yanqiu saw hope when Chunlai appeared, for the girl was all the reason anyone needed for Chang'e to exist. Like a grieving widow clinging to her only child, Xiao Yanqiu knew that her legacy would live on so long as there was a Chunlai. That was her final compensation from the gods, the last comfort they held out for her. Chunlai had just passed her seventeenth birthday and was, strictly speaking, still a girl. But she had never really been a girl. In a way she had been born a woman, an enchanting woman, a bewitching woman, a woman who could plunge you into bottomless sorrow with a single look. That is not to say she was precocious. She was just born that way. Chunlai entered the golden age of the *Qingyi* in her seventeenth summer with a figure that had all the things it should have had and none it shouldn't. Her waist was graced with a natural glamour that lent her a bewitching quality. A unique and wondrous light sparkled in her eyes. She did not just look at something, she cast a glance — a sidelong one here, a wistful one there. Her eyes embodied the ideal of expressing a reluctant parting and a coquettish sadness of unknown origin. When they were in motion, one would think that she was expressing herself onstage, for she was endowed with a talent to bring the most dramatic pattern down to the level of daily life and the special ability to elevate quotidian movement to the stage. For Chunlai, the adolescent change of voice occurred so smoothly that no one even noticed. For some performers, this change is the gate of hell, a career-ending barrier. They are in perfect singing form at their evening bath, only to discover upon awakening the next morning that demons have stolen their voices.

Good fortune smiled on Chunlai; everything, it seemed, had been prepared for her beforehand. She may have been a Chang'e understudy, but no one could deny that the spiritual light of the *Erlang* deity shone brightly down on her.

FIVE

SONGS ARE THE PRIMARY element of
Peking Opera. To speak the lyrics is
commonly called narrating an opera.
The performer atomizes the narrative, turns it into
countless fragments and details and transforms
the character's emotion, be that anger, happiness,
pain, or melancholy into a word, a smile, a glance,
or a flinging of the water sleeves, and then folds
these all back into the performance as a mono-
logue, an aria, a recitation, or a stylized gesture.
Only after these have been reassembled and
molded into alternating spoken and sung lines can
the actual rehearsals begin. First comes the ensemble rehearsal. An opera is not the work of one
person alone; it is, first and foremost, a study in
interpersonal relations. With so many performers
crowded onto a stage, they must learn to communi-

cate, to cooperate, to exchange ideas, and to take others into consideration. This carefully conducted process is the ensemble rehearsal. But it does not end there. The performers also need to develop a connection with the orchestra, with the gongs, the drums, and other instruments. How could anything called "opera" exist without the winds, the strings, and the percussion? Bring all the instruments together, and you have what is called the sound rehearsal. But there is yet more, the dress rehearsal, which approaches an actual public performance, as the actors play to a virtual audience. The headdress must be worn, the face must be painted, and everyone plays a part as if it were a real performance. Only when that is done can the curtain for the big show be raised.

Nearly everyone noticed that from the first day of opera narration, Xiao Yanqiu appeared to be trying a bit too hard, working too much. She had kept up with her routine, but she was, after all, a forty-year-old woman who had been away from the stage for two decades. Her unyielding work ethic, in contrast to the rashness of the young, was like a river, flowing east in the spring and displaying defiance and dignity. Yet it was hopelessly clumsy, with giant eddies and swirls that fought to turn back at the moment of merging with the ocean. It was an exhausting struggle, presenting the illusion of swimming against the tide, an involuntary downward slide, an unstoppable flow. Truly the passage of time is like water seeking lower ground; no matter how hard you try, the sad reality is that spilled water cannot be recovered. You strain to drag the ox by the tail, only to end up having it pull you into the water.

By the time of the opera narration, Xiao Yanqiu had successfully shed ten pounds. She was not losing weight so much as clawing it off, with earnestness and considerable pain. It was a battle of stealth, devoid of gunpowder, but producing significant casualties nonetheless. Her body was now her enemy, and she carpet bombed it with an avenging madness, all the while closely monitoring the situation. During those days, she was not only a bomber jet, but also an accomplished sniper, as, rifle in hand, she watched her body closely. It was her ultimate target, and she unflinchingly pulled the trigger whenever the slightest movement caught her attention. She stepped on the scales each night to see if she had met the strict, self-imposed demand of daily weight loss. She was determined to claw off twenty-five pounds, returning to her weight of twenty years before, for she was convinced that, so long as she shed those twenty-five pounds, her life of that period would return. The morning light of those days would once again cast her peerless figure onto the earth.

It was a long, cruel battle. Liquids, sugar, lying down, and hot foods are the four enemies of weight loss. For Yanqiu eating and sleeping were the magic words. She tackled sleep first, allowing herself only five hours a night; beyond that, she neither slept nor sat. Then she attended to what she put into her mouth. Neither rice nor water was allowed, especially hot water. All she ate were fruits and vegetables. Beyond that, like the insatiable Chang'e, she swallowed large quantities of pills.

Results were easy to come by at first. Her weight plummeted like stocks in a bear market. She lost the fat, but gained skin, which, like a found purse, hung from her body limply. This extra skin gave the illusion that she was more form than content. It was a strange impression, one both comical and loathsome. Worst of all, it showed most in her face. It gave her a widow's mien; staring at her reflection in the mirror, she felt every bit as dejected and despairing as a widow might.

But the true despair was yet to come. Once she

began to see the results of her weight-loss regimen, she suffered from light-headedness, a clear sign of malnutrition. She was becoming lethargic, was often dizzy and fatigued, grew anxious, and suffered from nausea and a lack of energy. With all this came a notable weakening of her voice. After the opera narration was behind them, preparations entered the dry-run stage, which meant an even greater depletion of energy. Her voice lost its power and sounded less steady, a bit shaky. As her breathing faltered, she had to tighten her vocal cords and, as a result, she sounded less and less like Xiao Yanqiu.

It never occurred to Yanqiu that she would one day make a fool of herself, and in front of so many people. While demonstrating a particular sequence for Chunlai, she "tattooed" her voice; in plain language, she croaked. Nothing is more embarrassing to someone who makes a living with her voice. What emerged sounded like the scratching of glass on glass or a hog on the back of a sow, not something that had come from a human throat. Every performer's voice tattoos once in a while, but Xiao Yanqiu wasn't just any performer, and she was mortified by all the eyes fixed on her. For her, those looks were not knives; no, they were poison, which draws no blood and causes no pain as it takes your life. She decided she must save face, that she had to recapture her dignity in front of them all. So, taking a deep breath to calm herself, she signaled to start over. But twice more she tried, and twice more she failed. Her throat itched horribly, as if a swarm of tiny bugs were crawling over it. She felt a cough rising in her throat, but managed to swallow it through sheer steeliness of will. Bingzhang, who was sitting off to the side, brought her a glass of water and, in an attempt to sound casual, said, "Here, take a break. Let's all take a break." But she refused the offer; to accept the glass at that moment would have been so unlike her. Turning to the performer in the role of Houyi the Archer, she said, "Let's try it again." This time she did not tattoo her voice, but only because she stopped before reaching for the high notes. Releasing a long sigh, she stood frozen.

No one dared come talk to her, no one dared even look at her. She forced herself to remain collected, but that too took its toll. People should never be too anxious to recover their dignity after a blunder; sometimes, the more they try, the greater the loss. Yanqiu swept her eyes over the people around her, but they seemed to have reached a tacit agreement to pretend that nothing had happened. This felt like a conspiracy, as cruel as an open accusation. She wanted to give it one more try, but her courage had left her. Bingzhang held up his glass and announced loudly, "Your teacher has a cold, so we'll stop here. We're done for the day." Xiao Yanqiu looked at him with teary eyes, fully aware of his good intentions; but what she felt like doing was rushing up, grabbing him by the collar, and giving him a couple of resounding slaps.

The room emptied out quickly, leaving only Xiao Yanqiu and Chunlai. Not daring to look at her teacher, Chunlai bent down and pretended to gather up her things. As she fixed her eyes on her student, Xiao Yanqiu marveled at the lovely profile, and at the girl's cheeks and chin, which held a luster normally seen only on fine china. She was lost in thought, as she silently repeated the question: Why don't I have that kind of good fortune?

The girl straightened up, unnerved by her teacher's gaze. "Come here, Chunlai," Xiao Yanqiu said. The girl stood still, unsure of what to do. "Chunlai," Yanqiu said, "I want you to sing that part for me." The girl gulped. How could she dare do that at a moment like this? All she could do was quietly say, "Teacher." Yanqiu moved a chair over and sat down. Though she was confused and anxious, Chunlai knew from her teacher's attitude that there was no getting out of it. So she calmed herself as best she could, struck a pose, and began to sing.

Xiao Yanqiu sat there studying the girl intently and listening carefully. But after a few moments her mind began to wander, and she glanced up at the full-length mirror on the wall. It was like a stage, cruelly showcasing her and Chunlai. Unconsciously, she began to compare the two of them. The contrast made her look so much older, ugly even. Back then she'd looked like Chunlai did now. Where had she gone? The saying that you mustn't compare yourself with others is so unkind. Yes, you mustn't compare yourself with others, but you also mustn't compare your present self with your former self. Mirrors will gradually reveal what is meant by "Green mountains cannot cover it up, and it will flow east with the river." Xiao Yanqiu felt her confidence slip away like water seeking lower ground. She recalled the elation she'd felt at the beginning of her comeback, and realized that the happiness would, like a puff of smoke or a passing cloud, vanish without a trace. Her resolve wavered and she considered withdrawing; but she couldn't. Chunlai, of course, had more to learn, but in broad terms it would not take the girl long to surpass her. Given her youth, there was no limit to what she could do one day, and this thought brought Xiao Yanqiu waves of sorrow and pain. She knew she was jealous.

Looking back, Xiao Yanqiu had suffered the consequences of jealousy for two decades, though she had not been jealous of Li Xuefen — never, not for a single day. Now, however, as she looked at her student, jealousy was unavoidable. It was the first time she'd experienced the lethal power of that emotion and it was as if she was seeing blood flow. She hated herself for being jealous, and could not permit herself to be this way; she decided to punish herself by digging her fingernails into her thigh. The harder she dug, the more she had to control herself, and the more she tried to control herself, the harder she dug. In the end, the sharp pains in her thigh brought an eerie sense of release.

Xiao Yanqiu stood up, determined to help Chun-lai rehearse, vowing to give the girl all she had to offer, leaving out nothing. Standing in front of Chunlai and holding her by the hand, she explained things patiently and corrected what needed to be changed, from her gestures to the look in her eyes. She proceeded little by little, determined to transform the girl into the Xiao Yanqiu of twenty years before. A setting sun cast the giant shadow of a plane tree on the window, caressing the glass and murmuring encouragement. The rehearsal hall grew darker and quieter, but neither teacher nor student thought to turn on the lights. Each gesture, each movement was repeated over and over in the dim light. As Yanqiu tended to every detail, down to the last knuckle of each finger, her face was mere inches from Chunlai, whose sparkling eyes were extraordinarily bright in the dim hall, enchanting and gorgeous. Xiao Yanqiu suddenly felt as if it was she herself who was standing before her, the lovely, graceful Xiao Yanqiu of two decades earlier. She was mystified; it was like a dream, like gazing at the moon in the river. Everything in front of her was uncertain and illusory. She stopped and cocked her head to fix her unfocused, almost misty gaze on the girl. Not knowing what was happening to her teacher, Chunlai also cocked her head to study Xiao Yanqiu, who moved behind her, cupped the girl's elbow with one hand and held the tip of her small finger with the other. She stared at Chunlai's left ear, her chin nearly pressing against the girl's cheek, so close that Chunlai could feel the warm, moist breath from her teacher's nose. Xiao Yanqiu freed her hands and, without warning, caught Chunlai in an embrace. Her arms seemed to have a mind of their own. They held the girl tightly, crushing Yanqiu's breasts against Chunlai's back; Yanqiu then rested her face on the nape of her student's neck. Stunned by what was happening, Chunlai did not dare move, not even to breathe. But a brief moment later, she was inhaling and exhaling great gulps of air and, with each one, her breasts brushed against the arms that held her. Yanqiu ran her fingers slowly over the girl's body, like water splashed on a glass desktop, flowing in all directions. Chunlai came to her senses when the fingers reached her waist. Not daring to shout, she pleaded in a tiny voice, "Teacher, please stop."

Xiao Yanqiu regained her composure. It was like waking from a dream, after which she was overcome with shame and dejection, although she wasn't sure exactly what she had just done. Chunlai picked up her bag and ran out, leaving Xiao Yanqiu standing alone in the middle of the empty hall, the sound of her student's frantic footsteps echoing in her ears. She wanted to call the girl back, but knew there was nothing she could say to her at a moment like this. She was mortified. It was getting dark outside, but night had not yet taken over. She stood with her arms hanging limp, feeling lost, not knowing where she was.

On the way home, Xiao Yanqiu was struck by a feeling that it had been a bizarre day. The streets felt strange, so did the colors of the streetlights, and the way people walked. She felt like crying, but had no idea what there was to cry about. It is hard to cry when you don't know what for, and that thought brought a lump to her throat; that lump, inexplicably, sent pangs of intense hunger through her body. It was an insane yearning, as if a dozen hands had risen inside her stomach and pulled at it in all directions. When she reached a small roadside eatery, she decided to stop. With an unfathomable sense of hostility, she walked in. Then, menu in hand, she chose only greasy, oily dishes, and when they came, she wolfed down three huge meatballs with a vengeance. And she didn't stop there, but kept at it, chewing and swallowing until she could hardly breathe.

S I X

CHUNLAI CONTINUED to rehearse as before, giving away nothing in front of Xiao Yanqiu, except that she wouldn't look her in the eye. She listened to what Yanqiu said and did what she told her to do, but she refused to make eye contact. There was a tacit understanding between them, not the sort that exists between a mother and daughter, but the fatal, unspeakable kind that can exist between women.

Xiao Yanqiu had never imagined that such awkwardness could develop in their relationship, could become an issue between them. It was difficult to resolve because it was so elusive. She was eating again, but was tired all the time. Spreading through her body, fatigue was now everywhere, although she could not identify the source. The thought of quitting occurred to her several times, but she could not bring herself to do it. Twenty years earlier, something similar had happened, and she had considered suicide, but was unable to go through with it. Now she reproached herself for that weakness, for not having died back then. The abrupt end of one's golden years cuts more deeply than death. She had neither lived up to her desires, nor carried out her wish to quit; and now there was nothing she could do — wanting to cry, she had no tears to shed.

Chunlai acted as if nothing had happened, was always composed and relaxed; no wind blew, no grass swayed. She merely kept a proper distance from Xiao Yanqiu, who had come to fear her student, although she would never admit it. If the girl kept up this aloofness, Yanqiu felt, her own life would end; there could be no middle ground. What had been the point of standing at the rostrum, teaching for two decades, if Chang'e could not be reborn through Chunlai?

IN THE END, Xiao Yanqiu slept with the factory manager, a decision that finally put her mind at ease. It had always been a matter of when, not if. She didn't feel one way or the other about it; it wasn't a good thing, it wasn't a bad thing, just something people have done since time immemorial. What sort of man was the factory boss, anyway? Someone who had enjoyed power and become wealthy, and she would not have been upset if he'd been a disgusting man or if he'd forced her to do it. As it turned out, neither was the case. She wasn't shy about such things; better to be straightforward and frank than to act coy. If the show was to go on, then the audience had to feel it was worth their while; otherwise, why bother?

On the other hand, she didn't feel especially good about what she did, and that gnawed at her. From the hours of the banquet up to the moment she put her clothes back on, the factory boss had played the role of a great man, a savior even. But when she was standing there naked, it seemed to her that he had no interest at all in her body. What exactly is a boss? At the time, pretty girls were like goods on a shelf; if something struck a boss's fancy, he had only to signal with a nod and the clerk would take it down for him. So she stripped, and at that moment, the look in his eyes changed. The effects of her diet were plain to see and, as she could sense, plainly displeasing. He didn't even try to hide his disapproval. At that instant, she'd have preferred a greedy, lecherous man, a sex fiend even, for then she'd simply have been selling her body. But he wasn't. He was even more a man of stature and power as he climbed into bed — he leisurely lay down on the Simmons mattress and gestured for her to get on top. Once there, she did all the work. At one point, he seemed pleased with her efforts, for he moaned a couple of times, and muttered, "Oh yeah . . . oh, yeah." What does that mean? she wondered. A few days later, he put on a foreign porn flick before she serviced him, and it dawned on her that he was parroting the sound the porn stars made. Where sex was concerned, he had gone global.

What they did could hardly be called making love; it wasn't even sex. She was just trying to please a man, servicing a man, and she felt so debased that she thought about stopping. But sex is so toxic it doesn't let you quit just because you want to. She had never felt that way when making love with Miangua, so she just went through the motions, reproaching herself the whole time: this woman is a slut, pure and simple, she chided herself.

It was drizzling as she made her way home. The wet streets glistened, filling her eyes with reflections and refractions from the taillights of passing cars. The glittery reds seemed overheated and unreal, creating a deep sense of desolation. Surrounded by kaleidoscopic lights dancing on the surface of the street, she felt she'd been defiled that evening. Though she couldn't say how, exactly, she knew it wasn't physical. At the head of the lane she bent over and tried to throw up, but succeeded only in producing dry heaves, terrible-sounding and foul-smelling noises.

By the time she arrived home, her daughter was already in bed. Miangua was sunk down in the sofa with the TV on, waiting for her. She avoided his eyes, unable to bring herself to look at him. Instead, she went straight to the bathroom, head down, to shower. But the thought of how such unusual behavior might make him suspicious led her instead to the toilet, where she sat down, but with no results from either end. She examined her body, front and back, to make sure there were no telltale signs before she felt confident enough to leave the bathroom. Despite her fatigue, she put on an energetic show so her husband would not detect anything. But he did. Wondering why she was in such high spirits, he asked, "Have you been drinking? Your face is red."

Xiao Yanqiu's heart skipped a beat. "You're seeing things," she said as lightly as she could manage.

"No, it is red," he insisted.

The conversation was heading somewhere she didn't like, so she changed the subject: "Where's the girl?"

"Went to bed a while ago."

She still couldn't face him, for his gaze would have been her undoing. "Go on to bed. I'm going to take a shower." She avoided the word "sleep," but "go to bed" said the same thing. Out of the corner of her eye she saw that he was rubbing his hands gleefully. For no apparent reason, she felt a stabbing pain in her chest.

Once in the shower, Xiao Yanqiu turned up the water until it nearly scalded her. That was what she wanted, to hurt herself. The pain, tangible and real, was mixed with a subtle pleasure, bordering on self-abuse. She let the water run as she rubbed herself vigorously, digging deep into her body with her fingers, as if wanting to extract something from it. Afterwards, she went into the living room to sit on the sofa, her skin bright red and tender. At around eleven o'clock Miangua walked in, wrapped in a towel. Obviously he hadn't gone to bed. "You look preoccupied. Did you find a purse on the street?" he said, wearing a hopeful smile. No response. "Hey," he said, incongruously, "it's the weekend."

Yanqiu shuddered and tensed, but did not move, so he sat down and snuggled up to her, his lips touching her earlobe. When he bit down gently and reached for the familiar place, she reacted, surprising even herself, by pushing him away so hard he fell off the sofa. "Don't touch me!" she screamed. It was a sound that scratched the quiet night, abrupt and hysterical. Miangua was staggered, at first embarrassed, then angry; but he did not want to disturb the oppressive silence. Her chest rose and fell like a sail that has caught the wind. Tears welled in her eyes; staring at her husband, she cried out, "Miangua."

It was a sleepless night. Yanqiu stared wide-eyed into the darkness. One eye looked to her past, the other to her future, but all she could see was darkness. Several times she nearly reached out to rub her husband's back, but she stopped herself. She was waiting for the day to break; once dawn came, yesterday would be over.

WHEN SHE WASN'T rehearsing, Chunlai was quiet as a glass of water. During breaks, she'd sit off by herself, her long, curved eyebrows raised, her luminous eyes darting here and there, looking both alluring and at ease. She had a quiet beauty with an easy grace, and her movements gave the impression of a frail willow swaying in the wind. But girls like her could erupt without warning; she could raise a three-foot wave on a windless day, and the news she brought on one particular day was like thunderbolts crackling above Xiao Yanqiu's head.

Shortly before the sound rehearsal, Bingzhang summoned Xiao Yanqiu to his office. He looked very unhappy. Chunlai was sitting there reading the evening paper. The girl's presence told Xiao Yanqiu that something had happened.

"She's leaving," Bingzhang said.

"Who's leaving?" Xiao Yanqiu was confused. She glanced at the girl, clearly puzzled. "Where to?"

Chunlai stood up, but was still reluctant to look at her teacher. She stared instead at the tips of her shoes, reminding Xiao Yanqiu of what she herself had been like twenty years before, when she had stood at Li Xuefen's bedside. But what they were thinking and feeling at each of those moments could not have been more different. After a long pause, Chunlai spoke up. "I'm leaving," she said. "I'm going to be on TV."

Xiao Yanqiu heard every word but understood nothing. A discordance existed between those two statements. This was bad news, but just how bad she could not be sure. "You're going where?"

Finally Chunlai showed her hand. "I don't want to be an opera singer any longer."

Now Xiao Yanqiu understood. She sized up her student before inclining her head and asking, "What is it you don't want to do?"

Again the girl fell silent, leaving Bingzhang to explain things to Yanqiu. "One of the TV stations needed a host, so she applied. That was a month ago. She had her interview, and she got the job."

Xiao Yanqiu recalled seeing ads placed by the TV station in the evening paper during the narration phase. It had, in fact, been a month, and the girl had, without a word, gone about securing the job. Stunned by the news, Yanqiu swayed, as if being pulled off her feet. Not knowing what she ought to do or say, she reached out for Chunlai's shoulder, but quickly withdrew her hand. By then she was breathing heavily. "Do you have any idea what you're saying?"

Chunlai looked out the window, but said nothing.

"Don't even think about it!" Xiao Yanqiu said, raising her voice.

"I know how much time and energy you've spent on me, but I've worked very hard to get where I am today. So don't stand in my way."

"Don't even think about it."

"Then I'll quit the academy."

Yanqiu raised her hands in a meaningless gesture. She looked first at Bingzhang, then at Chunlai. Her hands began to tremble; heartbroken, she grabbed the girl's lapels. "You can't," she said softly. "Don't you know who you are?"

"Yes, I do," Chunlai answered, her eyes lowered.

"No, you don't!" Yanqiu said, shooting pains stabbing her heart. "You don't know how good a *Qingyi* you are. I ask again, do you know who you are?"

The corners of the girl's mouth twitched, like an attempted laugh, but there was no sound. "The Chang'e understudy."

"I'll go talk to them. You'll be Chang'e and I'll be your understudy. Please, you mustn't leave."

Chunlai looked away. "I can't take the role away from my own teacher."

She sounded as determined as she'd been a moment before, but now seemed to leave a bit of room for negotiation.

Yanqiu grabbed the girl's hands. "You won't be taking it from me. You have no idea how wonderful you are, but I do. It's not every day a *Qingyi* is born. Wasting talent like yours would incur heaven's wrath! You'll be Chang'e, and I'll be your understudy. Promise me." She covered the girl's hands with her own and repeated urgently, "Promise me."

Chunlai raised her head to look at her teacher, something she hadn't done in a long time. Xiao Yanqiu returned her gaze, studying the look in her student's eyes; she saw doubt and misgiving, which told her she was prepared to make a fresh start. Yanqiu fixed her attention on the girl, as if the look in Chunlai's eyes would vanish if her gaze left the girl's face. Bingzhang, who was also watching the girl, detected a subtle change. He was sure he was right; he now knew exactly what to say to the girl and how to say it. So he gestured for Yanqiu to leave, but she was immobile, trancelike. Not until he laid his hands on her shoulders did she return to reality. On her way out the door she stopped to look back. "Go on, now," Bingzhang said softly. "Go on."

Xiao Yanqiu returned to the rehearsal hall,

where she stared at the window in Bingzhang's office. It was now the window to her life. The rehearsal was over and the hall was deserted, leaving her the lone figure in the large, now empty space to wait anxiously. Late-afternoon sunlight streamed in, filling the air with a soft orange glow and a filigree of dust motes that lent an uncanny warmth to the hall. Leaves on the potted plants seemed to grow bigger under the setting sun, their outlines blurred. Yanqiu paced up and down, hugging herself; then the window opened to reveal Bingzhang's head and arm. She could not make out his face, but she saw him wave vigorously. Then he balled up a fist, which was the sign she'd been waiting for. She steadied herself by holding on to the practice bar against the wall, tears wetting her eyes, before she slid to the floor, where she sat and cried. How close she'd come to seeing all her efforts wasted; she felt as if she'd survived a disaster. They were happy, comforting tears. Supporting herself with her hand on a chair to stand up, she then sat down and sobbed, savoring a feeling of consolation. As she dried her eyes she reproached herself for not having been more upfront with Chunlai when the opera cast was formed. If the girl had had a role to play, she'd not have gone looking for other work.

Xiao Yanqiu asked herself why she hadn't handed over the role at the beginning; why, at her age, she was still fighting over a *Qingyi* part. Why had she refused to accept the role of understudy? This was so much better. Now Chunlai could take her place. Chunlai was her second self. As long as Chunlai gained the fame she deserved, Yanqiu's lifework could be passed down through her. As these thoughts coursed through her mind, she felt she'd shed a heavy burden; the pressure and the gloom in her heart vanished. Give it up, give it up completely. She heaved a long, deep sigh, feeling suddenly reinvigorated.

Dieting is a lot like illness. Getting well can be like extracting thread from a silkworm cocoon, whereas falling ill is like the toppling of a mountain. Xiao Yanqiu had been off her diet only a few days when the red needle on her scale bounced back, dredging up more than a pound, like a free gift with each purchase. She'd been in a better mood for days, but as her weight returned, so did her regrets. An opportunity she'd fought so hard for was lost almost before she knew it, a realization that led to a new and crippling sadness. She would stare at the needle on her scale, and her mood would plummet if it edged upward. But she knew she mustn't allow herself to grieve over the results; she had to beat back the sorrow as soon as it began to form, pinch off every last trace of it. At first, she had thought that her promise to give up the Chang'e role would have a calming effect. But no, her desire to be on stage was stronger than ever. Be that as it may, she'd made a promise in front of Bingzhang, and that promise was like a sword that cut her in two. One half remained on the shore, while the other half was submerged in water. When the water self tried to come up for air, the shore self unhesitatingly pushed her down even farther. The shore self could feel the underwater self fighting for air, while the water self witnessed the cold cruelty of murder. The two women's eyes turned red from anger as they glared at each other. Xiao Yanqiu struggled both in the water and on the shore until she was utterly exhausted. So she decided to gorge herself, like a drowning person gulping down water. Her weight shot up; the regained pounds not only betokened her promise to Chunlai, but effectively stopped her from coveting the role. For the first time in her life Yanqiu realized that she could really eat, that she had an amazing appetite.

Everyone spotted the changes in Xiao Yanqiu, a taciturn woman who had given up dieting just when her efforts were beginning to show results. No one recalled hearing her talk about what she was up to, but they saw her face regain its luster and her voice rediscover its depths. Some assumed she had not recovered from "tattooing" her voice that time, for a proud woman like Xiao Yanqiu did not give up easily. But the abandoned diet was not the greatest change in her. Nearly everyone noticed that she took herself out of the picture once the full cast rehearsal started. For all intents and purposes, Chunlai was the only one rehearsing now, while Xiao Yanqiu sat in a chair facing the girl to prompt and occasionally correct her. Xiao Yanqiu looked happy, too happy, in fact, as if she had snatched the sun out of the sky and stored it in the fridge at home. Given the circumstances, she had no choice but to put on a show, to overact. As she devoted all her energy to Chunlai, she looked less like a performer and more like a director, or, to be more precise, Chunlai's personal director. No one knew for sure what she was up to; they had no idea what was ripening and flowering in her head.

Every evening she dragged herself home, exhausted. The fatigue lingered, roiled, and flooded through her body, like thick, suffocating smoke from burning leaves after an autumn rain. Even her eyes were tired; they would lock onto something and stay there, too weary to move on. She often stood up straight and breathed in deeply to rid her chest of the imagined smoke and mist. But the air never reached the right spot, so after a while she gave up.

The dazed look in Yanqiu's eyes did not escape the attention of Miangua, for whom his wife's lethargy was cause for serious concern. She had rejected him twice in bed already. Once she'd been cold and detached, the second time it was a case of nerves. The way she acted, you'd have thought that he didn't so much want to make love as to stab and make her bleed. He dropped a hint here and there, and sometimes was quite direct, but she remained oblivious. There had to be something terribly wrong with the woman's heart, for nothing seemed to touch her.

SEVEN

BINGZHANG CAME TO SEE Xiao Yanqiu when she was teaching Chunlai how to stand for maximum effect. Striking the right pose entailed not only the conclusion of one dramatic mood, but also the silent beginning of another; it had both its own logic and beauty. The most difficult task was finding the right measure of decorum, for that, ultimately, was what art was all about. Xiao Yanqiu had demonstrated the pose several times, and kept raising her voice until she was nearly shouting. She wanted everyone to take note of her enthusiasm, her even temper, and her willingness to show that she did not feel ill-treated, that she was at peace, as if her mood had been ironed out smooth. She was more than just the most successful performer around; she was also the happiest woman and sweetest wife in the world.

That was when Bingzhang showed up. Rather than step into the rehearsal hall, he waved to her through the window. This time he led her to the conference room, not his office, where they'd had their earlier conversation. The previous talk had been productive, and he hoped this one would be as well. In a pleasant, unhurried manner, he asked how the rehearsal was going, though it was obvious that this was not what he had in mind; unfortunately, beating around the bush was too ingrained a habit for him to do otherwise. For some reason, even though he was in charge of the drama troupe, he could not help being afraid of the woman sitting across from him.

Xiao Yanqiu sat with a single-minded concentration that was exaggerated to the point of borderline hysteria, like a woman waiting to hear sentence pronounced. Noting her demeanor, Bingzhang knew he needed to be careful with what he was about to say.

Finally he got around to the topic of Chunlai, and then came straight to the point. He told Yanqiu that the young woman had previously decided to move on out of concern that she'd be unable to go on the stage and was unsure of her future, not because she'd really wanted to leave. A smile burst onto Xiao Yanqiu's face. "I have no objection," she said in full voice. "Really, I have no objection at all."

Ignoring her comment, Bingzhang continued with what he wanted to say: "I should have spoken to you earlier, but I was kept from doing so by meetings in town." With a self-deprecating smile, he continued, "My hands are tied, as you know."

Yanqiu swallowed and repeated herself. "I tell you, I have no objection."

He gave her a cautious look. "We held two special high-level organizational meetings over what we consider a very serious matter," he said, "and I want to see what you think —"

Yanqiu jumped to her feet, so fast she even frightened herself. Again she smiled. "Really, I have no objection."

Bingzhang stood up and asked warily, "Have they spoken to you already?" She stared blankly, not knowing what "they" were supposed to have "spoken" to her about. Biting his lower lip, Bingzhang blinked nervously, filled with things to say, but unable to begin. Finally, he mustered up the courage to stammer, "We held those two meetings, and, we thought — they thought — it would be better for me to talk to you. You will take half the role . . . though naturally, we'll understand completely if you think it's a bad idea. But you will play half, Chunlai will play the other half. Do you think this will . . ."

She did not hear what came after that, though she had heard every word up till then. At that point, she realized that for days she'd been operating under false assumptions, from which she had been making plans. No one in authority had spoken to her. Putting on an opera was such a huge event, how could she decide which play to perform or who to play which role? Everything had to be finalized by the organization. She'd been thinking too highly of herself and overestimating her authority. One person getting half the role was the sort of decision the organization would inevitably make. That was how they always did it: one role, two performers. She was so happy she broke out in a cold sweat. "I have no objection," she gushed. "Honest, I have absolutely no objection."

Xiao Yanqiu's quick and easy agreement came as a surprise to Bingzhang. He studied her carefully and breathed a sigh of relief when he saw that she was sincere; he wanted to praise her, but could not find the words. Not until much later did he ask himself how he had come to utter a phrase that no one had used for decades. "Your consciousness has been raised," he'd said. She nearly shed tears of joy on her way back to the rehearsal hall, as she recalled the afternoon when Chunlai had talked about leaving and the words she'd used to convince the girl to stay. She stopped to look back at the conference room door. Although she'd told Chunlai in front of Bingzhang that she would be her student's understudy, obviously he had not taken her seriously. To him, apparently, she was just farting in the wind. And he was right, Yanqiu told herself. A vow from a woman like me is just that, a fart in the wind. No one believes a woman like me, not even me.

A wintry gust blew into the hallway and picked up a slip of paper, which immediately assumed the wind's form and its substance. The wind blew past Xiao Yanqiu, causing her to shiver. The paper itself was like a *Qingyi* in the wind, drifting yet wistful, until it was tossed into a corner by the wall. When another blast followed, it quivered, as if both seeking and trying to avoid the wind. That slip of paper was a sigh from the wind.

The weather turned bitterly cold as the opening approached. At moments like this, the factory boss showed his true mettle as a media manipulator. At first, there were occasional reports in the media, but the heat was turned up as the day drew near, until all the media outlets, big and small, had joined the clamor. The noise of popular opinion created its own mood, almost as if *The Moon Opera* had, bit by bit, become part of the people's daily life, the sole focus of attention by society in general. The media created a peculiar buzz, telling people that "everyone is waiting anxiously." Using the seductive countdown method, these expressions of public opinion reminded people that everything was ready, everything but the east wind, that is.

The voice rehearsal was nearly over, and Yanqiu had visited the toilet several times. She had sensed something was wrong as she crawled out of bed that morning, overcome by nausea. But she refused to dwell on her discomfort, since she'd felt much the same back when she was taking all those diet pills. But on her fifth visit to the toilet, she was troubled by feelings she could not describe; her only certainty was that she had something important to do. Her bladder felt full, yet each time she tried to urinate, nothing came. All the time she was in the toilet she thought about that important thing she hadn't yet done, but still could not say what it was.

The nausea returned when she got up to wash her hands. This time the sour taste drew her back to the toilet, where she threw up several times before stopping abruptly. Ah, now she remembered. She finally remembered. She knew exactly what she hadn't done over the past few weeks. Breaking out in a cold sweat at the realization, she stood at the sink and counted back. Today was the forty-second day since Bingzhang had first talked to her. Since then she'd been so busy with rehearsals she'd lost sight of a woman's most important monthly concern. In truth, she hadn't forgotten anything; the damned thing hadn't come. Now she recalled that crazy night with Miangua forty-two days earlier. She'd been so pleased, so elated, that she'd forgotten to take any precautions. How could she be so fertile? How could such a little escapade come to this? Women like me should never let ourselves be too happy, for if we are, then what should happen will not, and what should not happen will make a spectacle of us. Instinctively covering her belly with her hands, she felt shame, but that quickly subsided and was replaced by uncontrollable rage. The opening night was only days away. How had she failed to squeeze her legs together that night? Staring at herself in the mirror above the sink, she wrapped up her situation with a single comment, patterned after the coarsest of women, in the foulest language she knew: "Fuck me, a slut who can't even keep her legs closed!"

What was growing in her belly became her most urgent consideration. She counted the days again and felt a chill travel all the way down to her calves. Nothing could save her if she threw up on stage during the performance. The best solution was, of course, a surgical procedure, for that was clean and thorough and would solve all her problems. But surgery had its downside; pain, of course, but pain wasn't the worst of it. Not only would it take too long for her to recover, but she might well once again "tattoo" her voice on stage. Five years earlier she'd had an abortion, and it had taken a tremendous toll on her body, requiring almost a month to recover. She could not have another one. Pills were her only choice. They would abort the fetus quietly, and she would only need a few days' rest. She stood vacantly at the sink a while longer before leaving the toilet and heading straight for the main entrance. Xiao Yanqiu was fighting for time — not with anyone else, but with herself. Each day gotten through was one day saved.

Later that same day she held six small white tablets in her hand, with the doctor's instructions to take one in the morning and one in the afternoon for two days, then two on the third morning. When they were all gone, she was to see him again. The tablets had a lyrical name — Stopping the Pearl — as if such a lustrous object were slowly taking shape in her belly and hindering her from doing what she wanted. No wonder there were fewer poets and playwrights these days; they were all busy giving names to pills and tablets. Sadness surged up inside as she gazed at the tablets in her hand. A woman spends her life in the company of these things, something that started with Chang'e, who stole the elixir of immortality and flew to the moon. Now she, Xiao Yanqiu, had to follow in Chang'e's footsteps. Medicine is truly strange, one of life's oddest conspiracies.

Though she lived some distance from the hospital, she decided to walk home. Along the way, she grew angry at herself, but even more so at Miangua. By the time she arrived home, she was no longer just angry, she was filled with loathing. She walked in the door, gave him a nasty look, and went to bed without eating or washing up.

Yanqiu chose not to ask for sick leave, for abortion was not something to be proud of, and there was no need to spread the news. But she reacted badly to the Stopping the Pearl tablets: she was bilious and felt so light-headed it was as if she had just returned from the moon. With great difficulty, she managed to make it through a day of rehearsal, but her loathing was doubled; it penetrated the marrow of her bones. The homecoming scene that night was a repeat of the day before, except that the atmosphere was even colder. Her face was darker and more menacing than ever as she walked in the door. Like the preceding day, she didn't eat, drink, or wash up, and she didn't say a word before going straight to bed. The house felt different. For Miangua, a wintry wind had gathered at the door and was slipping in through a crack; he stood there listening for a while, unaware of what had happened and not knowing what to do about it.

But Xiao Yanqiu did not sleep. Miangua heard her sigh late at night, when all was quiet. She took in a breath and held it, as if not wanting him to hear, but she wasn't fooling anyone. He sighed too, but softly. Something was wrong, something was definitely wrong. He thought he could almost see the end of life.

Miangua began to feel nostalgic about the past, and when a person does so, it can only mean that something is nearing its end. He and Xiao Yanqiu were not a good match — like a pigeon settling into a magpie's nest. He'd come into her life when she was in dire straits. Now she was going back on the stage, becoming a star again. Where does Chang'e fly except up to the heavens? Sooner or later she would soar back into the sky, and it wouldn't be long before their home was turned upside down. He was reminded of her abnormal behavior over the past few days and could only sneer at the dark night.

Xiao Yanqiu took the last two tablets the following morning and sat at home waiting quietly. At nine, she went to the hospital with a stack of sanitary napkins. The doctor told her to take more tablets, this time three little white hexagons. She swallowed them all and walked around for a while before again sitting down to wait. The spasms began slowly, with increasing frequency. Bending over in the chair, she panted.

"What are you sitting here for?" the doctor said sternly when he came out. "It takes four hours. Go outside and run around or jump or do something. Don't just sit here!"

So she went downstairs, but the pain was so intense it felt as if something were gnawing at her insides. It was becoming unbearable, and she wished she could find a place to lie down. Not daring to go back upstairs, she knew as well that she could not hang around the hospital entrance, in case she ran into someone she knew; that would be too great an embarrassment. So, unable to hold out any longer, she decided to go home. Their place was empty, as were all the flats in the building. And as she stood in the living room, recalling what the doctor had said, she decided to jump, to stir things up a bit. So she took off her shoes and leaped into the air; her heels landed with a thud, frightening and energizing her at the same time. She listened intently before jumping again and landing with another thud. Encouraged by the thumps on the floor, she kept it up. The more she jumped, the greater the pain; the greater the pain, the more she jumped. The jumps accompanied the pain; the pain accompanied the jumps. She leaped higher and higher, and her spirits soared. A singular sense of contentment and relaxation spread over her; this was an unexpected reward, and an unforeseen pleasure. She took off her coat, laid it on the floor, and leaped and twisted as if her life depended on it. Her hair came loose and flailed wildly in the air, like ten thousand gesticulating hands. She felt an urge to shout, to scream, but knew it wouldn't help if she did. By this time she had forgotten why she was jumping.

Now she was just jumping, jumping to hear the thuds, jumping to feel the floor groan beneath her feet. Xiao Yanqiu was deliriously happy. She rose into the air; she was flying. Finally, physically drained, her last ounce of strength used up, she sprawled on the floor as tears of happiness flooded her eyes.

Downstairs, a shopkeeper wondered what all the noise was about. Sticking her head out the door, she muttered, "What's going on up there?" Her husband, who was counting cash, grunted without looking up, "Renovating, I suppose."

Around noon, the pearl slid from Xiao Yanqiu's body. With the bleeding the pain stopped, and with the disappearance of the pain she was more relaxed; she experienced an intoxicating relief. Exhausted, she lay down on the bed to savor that intoxication, the respite from pain, and the fatigue. Intoxication took her to a different realm, the respite from pain brought understanding, and the fatigue was itself a sort of beauty.

She fell asleep.

Xiao Yanqiu slept for a long time and was visited by fragmented dreams, disconnected bits and pieces, like moonlight reflected on the surface of water, flickering, crowding, and refracting, impos-

sible to piece together. She knew she was dreaming, but was unable to wake from her dreams.

"Slam!" Miangua was home from work. That afternoon, now that he was back home, he began acting strangely. He was careless, and nothing pleased him. Banging into this and dropping that, he filled the house with loud noises. Yanqiu thought about getting up to talk to him, but she had to abandon the idea. For she was too weak. She rolled over and went back to sleep.

She could tell that something was seriously wrong. But the truth of the matter is that by the time someone sees that something is seriously wrong, the severity of the situation has already progressed further than anyone could have imagined. Yanqiu's daughter finally drew her attention to the problem. That evening she came into the bathroom and asked, "What's up with Daddy these days?" She said it with an innocent look, which could only mean that she knew everything. The question shocked Yanqiu back to reality. She saw, in her daughter's eyes, her own lack of focus and the potential crisis the family faced. So after rehearsal the next day, she dragged herself to the market to buy an old hen and some imported ginseng. It was getting cold, and Miangua, who was out in the ele-

ments all day long, needed special nourishment. So did she. She decided she'd talk to him after dinner.

Miangua returned home, the wintry wind on his purple face. Yanqiu greeted him at the door, but was oblivious to the fact that her display of emotion was so uncharacteristic, so unlike a typical wife. He cast a suspicious glance and then looked away with increased apprehension. Before slouching over her homework on the balcony, the girl eyed her parents and then left them alone in the living room. Yanqiu looked over at the balcony before filling a bowl with chicken broth and carrying it to the dining table. Like a seedy tavern owner, she urged him eagerly, "Here, have some of this. It's especially nourishing in cold weather. Chicken broth with imported ginseng."

Miangua, sunk down in the sofa, didn't move. Instead, he lit a cigarette. There was laughter in the movement of his chest, but not in the odd expression on his face. Tossing the cigarette lighter onto the coffee table, he muttered, "Nourishing? Chicken broth? Imported ginseng?" Then he looked up and said, "Just what do you mean by nourishing? What for? So I can go out and walk the streets on a cold night like this, is that it?"

His words stung. And he knew it as soon as they were out. They implied that a man and a woman came together only for what they did in bed. His words had touched a nerve, though he'd blurted them out without thinking, because he was in a bad mood. He tried to smooth things over with a smile, but that made it even worse, for it gave him a harsh look. Like being splashed with cold water, Xiao Yanqiu was faced with the basest, most vulgar side of life. Wearing a long face, she spat out, "Suit yourself!"

She glanced again at the balcony and met her daughter's eyes. The girl quickly looked away and raised her head, as if lost in her own thoughts.

EIGHT

THE DRESS REHEARSAL was a roaring success. Chunlai performed the greater part of the opera and Xiao Yanqiu took over at the end, a sort of grand finale. It was a major event for teacher and student to appear on the same stage. Bingzhang, who was sitting in the second row, was so excited he had to strain to calm himself as he watched two generations of *Qingyi* perform. He sat there with his legs crossed, his fingers wildly tapping out the rhythm, like five little monkeys scampering down off a mountain. A scant few months earlier the troupe had been in terrible shape, and now they were actually putting on a performance. He was pleased for the troupe, for Chunlai, and for Xiao Yanqiu; but most of all, he was pleased for himself. He was, he believed, the big winner.

Xiao Yanqiu did not watch Chunlai's rehearsal. She stayed in the dressing room to rest, feeling unwell, until it was time to go on stage and sing the longest and most splendid aria, "The Vast Cold Palace," which Chang'e sings after flying heavenward and is alone in the palace of the moon. Moving from meandering and slow to a lyrical rhythm, and then to a strong beat that leads to a crescendo, it lasted a full fifteen minutes.

Chang'e is now in the celestial realm, where, with the Milky Way and the Morning Star disappearing, she looks down on the human world, as loneliness surges through her, highlighted by the green ocean and blue sky. Amid boundless heavenly benevolence, the loneliness fosters a bitter remorse. The remorse and the loneliness prey on each other, spurring the other on as, in the eternal night of the vast universe, stars sparkle, off into infinity, year after year. People are their own worst enemies; they want not to be human, but immortal. They are the cause of their own problems, not the solution. People, where are you? You are so far away. You are on the ground. You are deep in your own thoughts. You ingest the wrong elixir and live a life that cannot bear any reflection or reminiscence. Ingesting the wrong elixir is Chang'e's fate, it is a woman's fate, and it is humanity's fate. Humans are what they are. If they are fated to have only this much, they must not quest for more.

The *Erhuang* aria was followed by a flute dance, with Chang'e holding a flute brought up from the human world, and celestial fairies floating around her. Circled by the fairies, she projects helplessness, pain, remorse, and despair, as she gazes all around. Chang'e and the fairies strike a pose, and with that the curtain falls, ending *The Moon Opera*.

Bingzhang's original idea had been for Xiao Yanqiu and Chunlai to share half of the play during dress rehearsal, but Xiao Yanqiu was not sure her body was up to it. For, after taking the elixir, Chang'e has a brisk-tempo aria followed by a water sleeve dance with gestures that require exaggerated movements. Strength is essential for both the song and the dance. In the past, that would not have been a problem for Xiao Yanqiu, but today it was. It had only been five days since the abortion, which, though medically induced, had caused much bleeding. She was still frail and worried that her voice might not be up to it. Besides, it was only a dress rehearsal.

She had made the right decision, for the flute

dance alone proved to be too much for her. As soon as the curtain fell, she collapsed. The "fairies" were frightened, but she put on a brave face. Seated on the rug, she smiled and said, "I tripped, I'm all right." Then, instead of answering a curtain call, she headed for the toilet with a feeling that her body had taken a turn for the worse; something warm was dripping from down below.

When Yanqiu emerged from the toilet she was at once surrounded by cast members. Standing in front, Bingzhang smiled and gave her a thumbs-up. It was a heartfelt compliment. His eyes were moist. Xiao Yanqiu's Chang'e had been magnificent. He laid his hand on her shoulder. "You *are* Chang'e," he said.

Yanqiu smiled weakly, then spotted Chunlai, who was leaning against the factory boss, looking up and smiling radiantly as she said something to him. He walked with rapid, confident strides, a vibrant great man in disguise mixing with commoners. He smiled benevolently and nodded. Xiao Yanqiu knew at once that this was not a good sign, and her heart skipped a beat. But, with a smile on her face, she went up to greet them.

*

A SNOWSTORM HIT the city on the day *The Moon Opera* was to open. After the snowfall the sky cleared and bright sunlight shone down on the city, turning everything blindingly white. Like a gigantic cake submerged in thick butter, soft and warm, the snow-blanketed city was bathed in an unusual ambience, like a fairy tale or perhaps a birthday. Xiao Yanqiu lay in bed quietly gazing at the gigantic cake outside her window. She puzzled over the bleeding, which wouldn't stop. She was spent and needed her rest; she had to save energy for the stage, for every movement and gesture, for every word and every note.

By dusk the cake was ruined beyond recognition; the party was over, the guests had left, and messy, dirty dishes were strewn everywhere. The snow had melted in places, was piled up in others. Melted areas exposed the dirty, nasty, ugly, menacing face of the earth. After calling for a taxi, Yanqiu arrived at the theater ahead of curtain time. Makeup artists and technicians were there waiting. This was no ordinary day; it was the most important day of Xiao Yanqiu's life. She walked around the stage, front and back, greeting the technicians before going to the dressing room to check the props. Then she sat down quietly at her dressing table.

Looking in the mirror and slowly regulating her breathing, she examined herself closely. Like a traditional bride, she had to make herself up and dress with such care that she could be married off in glitter and splendor. Who the groom was she did not know, but the red curtain that had yet to be raised would be her head cover, her veil. Suddenly she was overcome by anxiety. The audience on the other side of that veil would be a mystery to her and she would be a mystery to them. Hidden behind it, she would be caught up in a paradoxical relation-ship with the outside world, each side wondering about the other. That notion made her heart beat faster, causing her thoughts to run wild.

After taking a deep breath to calm herself once more, she slipped on a long-sleeved gown and tied it around her waist before squeezing flesh-colored foundation cream into her palm and dabbing it evenly over her face, her neck, and the backs of her hands. This was followed by a layer of Vaseline. The makeup artist then handed her the red face paint, which she applied with her middle finger around the eyes and over the bridge of her nose. She paused to study the effect until she was satisfied. Then she brushed on powder and applied rouge on top of the heavy red face paint to highlight and brighten it. The outline of a *Qingyi* was beginning to emerge. Now for the eyes. With the tips of her fingers, she pushed the corners up toward her temples and painted both her eyelids and eyebrows When she removed her fingers, the skin around the corners sagged, leaving the outline of the eyes higher and lending the area an oddly seductive, almost fiendish look.

That done, she turned herself over to the makeup artist, who moistened a band to raise the brows and, adding a bit of discomfort, pull the sagging eye corners up. Then she wrapped another band around Yanqiu's head, over and over to hold the skin around the corners of her eyes in place, turning them into the bewitching and lively eyes of storybook foxes. The brows and eyes now done, the makeup artist pasted patches on Xiao Yanqiu's cheeks to transform her face into an oval shape. The completed image of a *Qingyi* materialized in the mirror after the addition of the bangs, the sheer second layer of clothing, the headdress, and a wig. Xiao Yanqiu stared at herself, hardly able to recognize the beauty looking back at her. Clearly, it was another woman from another world. That, she believed, was the real Xiao Yanqiu, her true self. She thrust out her chest and looked over her shoulder, discovering to her surprise that the dressing room was crowded with people, studying her with looks of wonder. Chunlai was standing right beside her. She'd been there all along, transfixed, finding it hard to believe that the woman beside her was her teacher, Xiao Yanqiu. Like magic, Yanqiu had transformed herself into a different person, and she knew without question what Chunlai was feeling at that moment: the girl was jealous. But Yanqiu said nothing, for at that moment she was not just anyone; she was her true self, another woman from another world. She was Chang'e.

The curtain went up, raising the red veil. Xiao Yanqiu spread her water sleeves, prepared to marry herself off. There was no single bridegroom; she was marrying the world and everyone in it. The bridegrooms in the audience all fixed their attention on the one true bride. Xiao Yanqiu stood in the wings as the gongs and drums sounded.

She hadn't expected the opera to be so short. She felt she'd just begun, had barely left the world, and now she had returned. At first, concerned about her stamina, she was somewhat nervous when she took to the stage; but she was quickly able to relax. She began to express, to confide, eventually forgetting herself, forgetting even Chang'e.

Turning the grievances in her chest into a long thin thread, she slowly unraveled it, entwining herself as she moved freely. She revealed herself to the world and the world applauded her in return. Gradually she lost herself; she was enthralled, sinking further and further into the opera.

For her they were two hours of joy, two hours of sobbing, two hours of exhaustive emotion, two riotously high-flying hours, two intoxicatingly merry hours, two sad and plaintive hours, two unbridled hours, two hours of dazed confusion. It was like two hours spent frolicking in bed. Her body and her heart were opened up, spread out, elongated, moistened, softened, loosened, and filled to the point of near transparency, brimming, as if on the brink of a climax. She felt as if she'd turned into a ripe grape, whose sticky juice would burst from a gentle slit and flow unimpeded, like a wish fulfilled. But the opera was finished. It was all over.

That other woman departed cruelly, leaving Xiao Yanqiu to be just herself again. She had been in perpetual motion, and now she couldn't stop; her body didn't want to. It wanted to go on, to sing more and perform more. She could not recall how she'd answered the curtain call, except that the curtain had come down like a dark face, like a man withdrawing just as she is reaching orgasm. She was heartbroken; she wanted to shout to the people below, "Don't go. Please don't go. Come back. Come back now."

The performance was finished and everything was over. For Yanqiu it was less a matter of exhaustion than of nervous energy still waiting to be released. Her anxieties were telling her to do something. Dejected and lost, she walked backstage, where Bingzhang stood waiting for her. He greeted her with open arms. She walked up and, like a mistreated child, threw herself into his arms. As she buried her face in his chest, she began to wail. He patted her on the back, over and over; he understood. He was blinking uncontrollably. But no one could know exactly how she felt, no one could know what she wanted to do at that moment; even she did not know. Chang'e had flown away, leaving Xiao Yanqiu alone in this world. At that moment she wished she could find a man and make passionate love. She looked up abruptly, unnerving Bingzhang with a face that, given the smeared face paint, was more ghostly than human. He did not expect to hear what she said next, and it was clear that he did not understand her after all. Looking at him coolly, she said, "I'm going to sing again tomorrow. Promise me I can sing again tomorrow."

Xiao Yanqiu gave four performances in a row, and would not yield, not to her student, not even, had they asked, to her own parents. It was no longer a matter of who was whose understudy. She was Chang'e, she was the true Chang'e. Xiao Yanqiu was unconcerned about the change in atmosphere in the troupe during those days, or how people looked at her. She had no time for any of that. When it was time for makeup, she sat calmly in front of the mirror to transform herself into someone else.

Following four days of fair weather, the afternoon sky suddenly turned overcast. The weather forecast was for a late-day snowstorm. In the afternoon the wind came, but no snow. Xiao Yanqiu was fatigued, her legs leaden, as if she had been trussed up. She developed a fever a little after three o'clock and was bleeding again, more than usual. It wouldn't stop. The fever came fast and spiked quickly. Chills ran down her back, while tugging pains developed in her thighs. Worried, she went to the hospital and registered at the gynecology department.

She had it all planned; she'd get a prescription

and rush back so as not to miss that night's performance. But this time the doctor held off on writing a prescription. Instead he asked many questions and put her through several tests. He looked somber, not to alarm her but not wanting to put her mind at ease either; it was as if to say, you're not about to die, but you do have a problem. Finally he spoke. "Why didn't you come earlier? Your uterine wall is badly infected. Just look at your blood count." He added, "You need an operation. I want you to admit yourself as a patient."

But Xiao Yanqiu was not in a bartering mood. "I'm not staying," she said firmly. "Can't it wait?"

The doctor looked at her over the top of his glasses. "The body won't wait."

"I'm telling you I won't stay."

The doctor picked up his prescription pad, wrote with a flourish, and said, "Let's at least deal with the infection. No matter how busy you are, you must do that. I'll arrange for a couple of IV bottles, then we'll see."

Yanqiu walked out into the lobby to check the clock. Not much time, but enough. The IV would be finished by five and she'd have time to eat something before getting to the theater around five thirty. She wouldn't miss anything. It might even be a good idea to rest while she was getting the IV, which meant that, for a while at least, she would stay in the hospital.

Yanqiu never expected to fall into such a deep slumber in the IV room, like the sleep of the dead. At first she'd planned only to close her eyes and rest awhile, but the room was so warm she fell fast asleep. She was so tired, her fever was so high. Besides, the curtain was closed around her, so how would she know from the artificial lighting how fast time was flying? She woke up, feeling better, as if her body had been freed. But when she asked the time, she flew into a panic. Ripping out the needle, she ran to the door, not even stopping to pick up her purse.

Outside it was already dark. Snowflakes, big, dense snowflakes were falling. Distant neon lights blinked on and off in the blanketing snow, turning the flakes into little whores who could worm their way into any spot, whereas the high-rises were towering, whoring men who seemed to sway in the illusory scene. Xiao Yanqiu tried to flag down a taxi, but they were all taken, and the drivers mockingly honked their horns at her. Too anxious to feel sick, she kept on, now revitalized. She ran, yelling and waving her arms.

Chunlai was finished with her makeup when Xiao Yanqiu stormed into the dressing room. Their eyes met, but Chunlai said nothing. In one of the classes Yanqiu had told her that a person disappears from the world after she is made up. You are no longer yourself. You don't know anyone and you don't listen to anyone. Yanqiu grabbed the makeup artist, wanting to tell her, wanting to tell everyone, "I am the true Chang'e. Only I can be Chang'e." But she didn't. She couldn't make a sound; all she could do was move her lips. At that moment, she wished that the Queen Mother of the West would descend from heaven and give her an immortality pill. Once she swallowed that, she would be transformed into Chang'e instantaneously, even without the aid of makeup. But there was no Queen Mother of the West, no one to give her an immortality pill. She turned to look at Chunlai, whose face was more beautiful than a fairy's. Now she was Chang'e. There could be only one Chang'e; anyone who was made up like that became Chang'e.

The drums and gongs sounded. Yanqiu watched as Chunlai went to the door. The curtain went up, and Yanqiu saw the factory manager sitting in the middle of the third row, smiling amiably like a great man, applauding slowly like a great man. The sight of him sitting there strangely calmed her. She knew that this time her Chang'e was dead. Chang'e's remorse ended on that snowy night in Xiao Yanqiu's fortieth year, cause of death unknown, at the age of forty-eight thousand.

Xiao Yanqiu returned to the dressing room and sat down wordlessly at the mirror. The applause from the theater made the room seem especially quiet. She stared at herself, her eyes unfocused, like moonlight on an autumn night. She had no idea what she was doing, as, zombielike, she picked up the dress with water sleeves and draped it over herself. She squeezed flesh-colored foundation into her hand and dabbed it evenly over her face, her neck, and the back of her hands. Then she asked the makeup artist to raise her eyebrows, wrap her head, apply the bangs, and put on the headdress. Lastly, she picked up her flute. All this she did calmly, so eerily quiet that the makeup artist felt a chill, the fine hairs on her back standing up. Terrified, she stared at Xiao Yanqiu with unconcealed apprehension, but Yanqiu stood up without a word, opened the door, and walked out.

Dressed only in a thin opera robe, Xiao Yanqiu walked out into the snow and arrived at the theater entrance, where she stood beneath a streetlight.

She glanced at the snow-covered street, counted a beat, and waved the bamboo flute. She began to sing, the same *Erhuang* aria, slow and meandering to a lyrical rhythm, and then to a strong beat, leading to a crescendo. Snowflakes swirled around her, and suddenly there was a crowd at the entrance, causing traffic to stop. More and more people arrived, crowding the street, but nothing, no one, made a sound. The people and cars seemed to have been blown to her on the wind, falling soundlessly like snowflakes, but Xiao Yanqiu was oblivious to it all. Another round of applause erupted inside the theater. She danced and sang. Finally, people noticed something dripping from her pant legs to the ground. The drops, black under the streetlight, fell on the snowy ground and created a series of black holes.

GLOSSARY

bodhisattva: in the West, a patron, an "angel"

Chou: the clown role in Chinese opera

consciousness: class consciousness; a Cultural Revolution slogan

Dan: the major female role in Chinese opera

east wind: a key element in Chinese lore

Egg (Dan) Nest: "Dan," with one character, means "egg"; another character, with the same pronunciation, is the opera role

Erlang: nephew of the mythical Jade Emperor, a deity with a third, true-seeing eye

great man: alludes ironically to historical figures, in particular Mao Zedong, who were referred to as "great"

Hualian: another name for a *Jing*, the male role with a painted face

Jing: the male role with a painted face in Chinese opera

Mo: the secondary male role in Chinese opera

Sheng: the major male role in Chinese opera

water sleeves: long, loose sleeves worn by opera singers that highlight stylized gestures

Xipi, Erhuang: tunes in the operatic repertoire are all named; the lyrics are added